Spencer Bishop was the last person on earth she'd expected— or wanted—to see...

In the years since she'd seen him, Natalie had managed to forget—or at least she told herself she had—how tall he was, how broad his shoulders were. How masculine he seemed. His green eyes looked darker and deeper than she remembered, almost sinister as he held her gaze without wavering.

Bishop eyes. Like his brother's. Her ex-husband.

She gazed up at him, the very sight of him—the memories of him—making her tremble. "I didn't do it," she whispered. "I didn't kill Anthony."

He didn't say anything. "You think I killed him," she whispered. "Just like the police do."

The irony of the situation was devastating. Natalie didn't know which was worse. Being suspected of a murder she hadn't committed, or facing the steely eyes of the man she'd once loved.

Dear Reader,

They're rugged, they're strong and they're *wanted!* Whether sheriff, undercover cop or officer of the court, these men are trained to keep the peace, to uphold the law. But what happens when they meet the one woman who gets to know the man *behind* the badge?

Twelve of these men are on the loose...and only Harlequin Intrigue brings them to you—one per month in the LAWMAN series. This month meet Spencer Bishop, an FBI man who's accustomed to finding out the truth. He's about to learn one truth that he's not quite ready to handle....

Be sure you don't miss a single LAWMAN coming to you in the months ahead...because there's nothing sexier than the strong arms of the law!

Regards,

Debra Matteucci
Senior Editor and Editorial Coordinator
Harlequin Books
300 East 42nd Street
New York, New York 10017

A Man of Secrets
Amanda Stevens

Harlequin Books

TORONTO • NEW YORK • LONDON
AMSTERDAM • PARIS • SYDNEY • HAMBURG
STOCKHOLM • ATHENS • TOKYO • MILAN
MADRID • WARSAW • BUDAPEST • AUCKLAND

For my mother, with love.

ISBN 0-373-22397-8

A MAN OF SECRETS

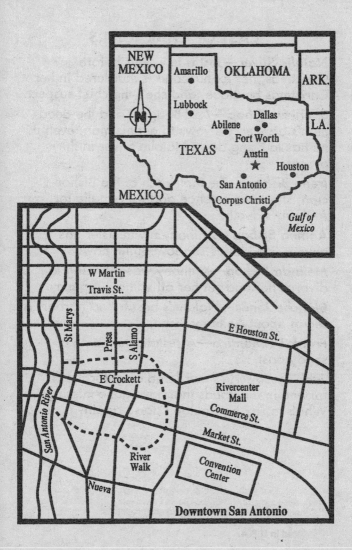

CAST OF CHARACTERS

Natalie Silver—Just a few days before Christmas, her ex-husband is murdered in her Christmas boutique, and she's the chief suspect.

Spencer Bishop—An FBI agent and the dead man's brother. He vows to get his man, even if he has to bring down Natalie Silver in the process.

Irene Bishop—The matriarch of the Bishop clan, she vows revenge against Natalie for Anthony's death.

Anthea Bishop—Anthony's twin sister has always lived in his shadow—until now.

Melinda Bishop—Anthony was planning to divorce her and cut her off without a penny.

Blanche Jones—Natalie's best friend harbors a secret about Anthony Bishop.

Frank Delmontico—A restaurateur with a shady past.

Jack Russo—He's murdered once for the fortune in diamonds that have gone missing. Who's to say he wouldn't do so again?

Chapter One

He was up to something. Natalie Silver twirled her glasses in one hand as she tracked her ex-husband's slow progress through her shop on San Antonio's famed Riverwalk. His presence seemed incongruous in the cheery warmth of Silver Bells, her potpourri-scented Christmas boutique.

Christmas music played softly in the background, and tiny white lights, trimming doorways and windows, glowed with subtle magic. But Anthony's presence reminded Natalie of darker times. Unpleasant times.

He picked up an Austrian-crystal snowflake and held it to the light, then laid it aside to admire a hand-carved wooden Christmas tree, meticulously detailed, done by a famous German craftsman. He left the tree and sauntered toward the Belgian angels.

"What exactly are you looking for?" Natalie finally asked.

Anthony looked up and gave her a cool smile. "I'll know it when I see it."

As he lifted his left hand to remove one of the angels from the shelf, the glint of sunlight flashing off his gold watch attracted Natalie's gaze. He wasn't wearing his wedding ring, she noted, feeling more wary by the moment. He'd been married to his current wife for six years—ever since he and Natalie had divorced—and the sudden absence of his wedding band seemed ominous to her somehow.

"Maybe if you told me who the gift is for, I could help you find something," she suggested. Not that she had any particular desire to be helpful to Anthony—or to any of the Bishops, for that matter—but the sooner he found what he was looking for, the sooner he would depart.

Of course, that notion wasn't exactly consoling since when he left, he would be taking her son with him for the evening. That alone was enough to fill Natalie with trepidation, but this new attitude of Anthony's... this new congeniality...

He was up to something, all right. Natalie hadn't yet figured out what, but she was very much afraid it had something to do with her son. In the six years since their divorce, Anthony had shown no interest whatsoever in Kyle, had done nothing more than have his secretary send the occasional birthday or Christmas card, along with an obligatory, impersonal check.

Even Irene, Kyle's grandmother, had kept her distance, and Natalie had begun to hope the Bishops were out of her life for good.

But a month ago, out of the blue, Anthony had called her to say he wanted to start spending time with Kyle on a regular basis. Since Anthony had legal visitation rights and he'd always paid his child support on time, there was nothing Natalie could do to prevent him from seeing her son—no matter how much she might wish to.

And besides, she knew Kyle was curious about Anthony. About all the Bishops. Because he *was* one.

"The gift is for the mother of one of my clients," Anthony explained. "She's very old and her son's been away for quite some time. I want to send her something that will help brighten her holidays."

Natalie slipped on her glasses and scrutinized him again. He looked the same—impeccably dressed in a dark, double-breasted suit, black hair combed straight back from a high forehead winged with heavy eyebrows, green eyes fringed with thick lashes, and a wide, generous mouth that could look either sensuous or cruel, depending on his mood.

Natalie had had the misfortune to witness both those moods on occasion, but this new persona—showing fatherly interest, concern for a client's elderly mother—was a side of Anthony she hadn't seen since he had caught her on the rebound and swept her off her feet nearly seven years ago in a whirlwind courtship that had left her breathless; and almost immediately filled with regrets.

Her ex-husband was a master of deception. He could fool most of the people most of the time, but he would never again dupe Natalie. She'd been taken in once by his lies, by his impersonation of a caring man, but she would never believe him again. Natalie knew too well what Anthony Bishop was capable of.

She walked around the counter and faced him. "Why don't you tell me what you really want?"

He gave her an innocent look. "I don't know what you mean."

"You know exactly what I mean. Why this sudden interest in Kyle?"

The dark eyebrows slowly rose. "I'm his father. Or had you forgotten the details of his parentage?"

"I'm not likely to forget anything concerning my relationship with you," she said bitterly. "But I can't help wondering why, after all these years, you suddenly want to be a part of my son's life."

"He's a Bishop."

Natalie's lips tightened but she said nothing.

Sunlight silvered the gray at Anthony's temples as he turned to study her. "Like it or not, Natalie, the boy's my heir. I have certain legal and moral responsibilities toward him, which I intend to start exercising. You may as well get used to it. In fact, I'd like for him to spend the Christmas holidays with me at Fair Winds."

Over my dead body. Images of her first and only Christmas at the Bishop mansion raced through Natalie's mind. She'd been a new bride—shy, insecure, and still heartbroken from a love affair gone bad. Her marriage to Anthony, who was fifteen years older than she, had been an act of haste, an impulsive, desperate decision that she had, even then, begun to regret.

But after that week at Fair Winds, the full weight of what she had done hit her. Anthony's cruelty—no longer masked by a warm, caring facade—his mother's coldness and his sister's bitter resentment of Natalie had made the holiday season almost unbearable for her that year.

And through it all, the conspicuous absence of Anthony's younger brother, Spencer, the Bishop Natalie had come to hate the most, had been a constant reminder of how stupid she'd been. How gullible.

She rubbed her temples now, trying to rid herself of the dark visions dancing in her head. "There is no way I'll let Kyle spend Christmas at Fair Winds."

"Are you sure about that?" Anthony wasn't looking at her, but was gazing instead at the pine armoire in which she kept the more expensive antiques and rare collectibles. He glanced over his shoulder. "Supposing you don't have a choice in the matter?"

A dark premonition slipped over Natalie. She shivered in spite of the seventy-degree weather San Antonio was enjoying. "What do you mean?"

"I mean, why don't you let the boy decide? Ask him where he wants to spend Christmas. Or...are you afraid of his answer?"

Anthony's taunt sent a spasm of anger shooting through Natalie, but it wasn't quite enough to dispel the fear that had suddenly seized her. She'd been nineteen when she'd first seen the Bishop mansion. Her own impression had been one of starkness, of a cold, sterile mausoleum completely lacking in warmth or love. But Kyle was only six years old. He could easily be swayed by the ostentatious grandeur of Fair Winds; and even more persuasive was his own sense of adventure.

The thought of not having Kyle with her for Christmas filled Natalie with the kind of aching loneliness she hadn't known in years. Her son meant everything to her.

"Kyle will be with me for Christmas," she said firmly. "And that's final. You may see him the day before or the day after, as per the custody agreement, but on Christmas Day, he *will* be with me."

Anthony looked on the verge of arguing with her. Then, for some reason Natalie could only guess at, he merely smiled and inclined his head. "Whatever you say, Natalie. In the meantime, I think I've found what I'm looking for."

His green eyes swept her in a manner so proprietary, so intimate, Natalie felt herself blushing. Slowly, his gaze left her face to travel downward and linger where the neck of her dark red cotton sweater dipped demurely, and downward still, tracing the lines of her short pleated skirt and the black opaque stockings encasing her legs.

When his eyes moved back up to meet her defiant gaze, Natalie felt as if she'd just been undressed—against her will. It wasn't a pleasant sensation.

"I'd like to have a closer look."

The deep, seductive quality of his voice startled her. *"What?"*

He motioned toward a piece in the armoire, but his eyes told her he meant something else. "I'm interested in the music box. The one with Saint Nick on top."

Leave it to Anthony to zero in on the *pièce de résistance* of her collection, the one item Natalie had been hoping to keep for herself.

"It's an Étienne," she explained, brushing past him to remove the delicate porcelain music box from the shelf. "An exact replica of the ones made in Paris before the war and used by the underground during the occupation to smuggle messages back and forth." She touched a spring, cleverly concealed by the intricate design of the piece, and a hidden compartment popped out. She gave him an ironic glance. "I remember how much you love secrets."

He grinned. "And how much you hate them."

With good reason, she thought. During their short marriage, Anthony had kept a lot of things from her, but the worst had been his affair with Natalie's best friend, the woman who was now Mrs. Anthony Bishop.

Anthony removed the music box from Natalie's hands. "How much is it?"

She named a figure that was twice as much as she'd planned to ask, but she knew her ex-husband could afford it.

He whistled, studying the music box at length. "I had no idea you could command that kind of price for a Christmas ornament."

"Only from my most discriminating customers," Natalie said dryly.

Both dark eyebrows rose at that. "Well, that's a challenge I can hardly refuse, now, isn't it? I presume that price includes gift wrapping?"

"Of course."

"And delivery?"

"Within the continental United States," Natalie said. "Shall I wrap it up for you?"

"Why not?" Anthony fished in the inside pocket of his coat and handed her a piece of paper. "Here's the address I want you to send it to. It's here in San Antonio, so I'd like for you to make arrangements to have it delivered today."

Natalie glanced up. "That'll cost extra. I'll have to hire a special courier."

Anthony shrugged. "I'll leave the details to you. As long as my friend's mother has her present by tonight."

"She will," Natalie assured him. "Now, will this be cash?"

He handed her a platinum credit card. When Natalie tried to take the music box from him, he nodded toward the door, where two women had just walked in. "Looks like you're a little shorthanded today. Why don't you go ahead and wait on your customers? I'm in no hurry."

Natalie could hardly believe her ears. In the old days, Anthony would have insisted on being served first. He would have thought it his due as a Bishop. Now he seemed content to browse while Natalie took care of her other customers. She didn't quite know what to make of this new attitude.

Something about him had changed, but then, some things never did. By the frank perusal he'd given her earlier, Natalie suspected her ex-husband still had a roving eye. She wished she could take pleasure in the knowledge that he and Melinda's marriage seemed to have gone sour, but none of that mattered in the least to her anymore. If it wasn't for Kyle, she would never want to see another Bishop as long as she lived.

By the time she finished with the barrage of customers who had suddenly descended on Silver Bells, Anthony was pacing the shop impatiently. He handed her the music box and glanced at his watch.

"I'm late for a meeting," he said. "I won't be able to wait for Kyle after all."

"But you were supposed to take him to the Spurs game tonight," Natalie protested. Not that she wanted Anthony anywhere near her son, but she didn't want Kyle to be disappointed, either. She didn't want Anthony turning up in her son's life only at *his* convenience.

"I'm afraid something's come up." He glanced over his shoulder, toward the front of the shop. Outside, a man in a loud print shirt had stopped to study the animated Santa's workshop scene in the display window.

Anthony turned back to the counter. "Can you speed this up?"

"I thought you weren't in any hurry."

"Well, I am now."

So the old Anthony *was* still lurking nearby. In a way Natalie was relieved.

Carefully, she placed the music box inside a silver carton embossed with her shop's logo—a pair of beribboned bells—and taped the delivery address to the counter so it wouldn't get misplaced.

"You're sure it'll go out today?" Anthony asked anxiously.

"I'll call the courier immediately," Natalie assured him, shoving her wire-rimmed glasses up her nose.

"Okay." He tapped the counter with one fist as he glanced over his shoulder again, and Natalie automatically followed his gaze. The man at the display window had moved on.

She said, "You don't have to worry. I'll take care of everything."

"I'm counting on that," said Anthony.

AS SOON AS NATALIE had a free minute, she called the courier, then picked up the silver carton containing the music box and carried it back to her workroom. Placing it carefully on her desk, she got out several sheets of bubble wrap and removed a shipping label from her desk drawer. But before she finished, the bells outside chimed again.

This time, the Bishop who walked through her door was one Natalie was delighted to see. Her six-year-old son came rushing in, pulling Blanche Jones behind him. Both of them were windblown and laughing.

Blanche, one of Natalie's closest friends, owned Blanche DuBois's, a vintage clothing shop on the third level of the same building that housed Silver Bells. An Italian restaurant, owned by a man named Frank Delmontico, occupied the ground level.

Blanche and Natalie had hit it off immediately, five years ago when Natalie first opened her shop, but Frank Delmontico still remained somewhat of a mystery man.

The two women often lunched in his restaurant and speculated about his past. Natalie thought he looked like a hit man for the Mafia, but Blanche insisted his tough, swarthy looks belonged to someone who had once sailed the high seas, a merchant marine perhaps, or even a treasure hunter.

Neither of them had ever asked him about his background, though, because Blanche, always the romantic, had said it was much more fun to create one for him. Think how disappointed they would be, she had pointed out, if he turned out to be an accountant.

Natalie thought Blanche one of the most interesting women she'd ever met, in both personality and appearance. She was not just pretty, but intriguing. Today she wore a crocheted sweater paired with a long lace skirt in winter white, beneath which peeked old-fashioned, lace-up boots.

Her thick dark hair was pulled back and held in place by an antique ivory comb her grandmother had given to her, and an exquisite cameo, tied with a satin ribbon, adorned her throat. Natalie thought that her own cotton sweater and plaid skirt must look positively drab by comparison.

"Well, you two sure look happy," she commented. Their laughter was contagious. The dark cloud that had been hanging over Natalie's head since Anthony's departure began to dispel.

Kyle grinned from ear to ear, displaying the gap where his two adult front teeth hadn't yet grown in. "I came in first, Mom!" he shouted, lisping a little on the word "first." "I won the Reindeer Run! I did what you told me. I closed my eyes and pretended I really *was* a reindeer. And it worked! It really worked! You should have been there!''

His excited tone contained not even a hint of censure, but Natalie felt a pang of guilt just the same. She *should* have been there. Being a single parent was hard enough, but owning and operating a small business spread her even thinner.

She'd wanted to take the afternoon off to watch Kyle run, but unfortunately, she'd had two deliveries arriving that day, coupled with the fact that one of her part-time clerks had been out sick all week. Michelle, who came in after school and worked until closing, wouldn't be in until later. This was Natalie's busiest time of year. There was no way she could close up shop, even for an hour or so. Kyle, bless him, seemed to understand. At least as much as a six-year-old could.

He tore off his windbreaker and puffed out his chest, proudly displaying the T-shirt he'd won.

''See? It says First Place, Reindeer Run.'' He pointed to the words, then looked up, beaming.

''All right!'' Natalie walked over and gave him a high five. Then she bent down and hugged him. ''I knew you could do it. You're fast as the wind!''

''The fastest kid in first grade, anyway,'' Blanche said.

Kyle squinted up at Natalie. ''Are you proud of me, Mom?''

''I'm always proud of you, sweetie.'' And it was true. Kyle could be a handful at times, and like his father, he had a secretive quality that could drive Natalie crazy. But most of the time, he brought her nothing but joy. Most of the time, she managed to forget that he was a Bishop.

"Did you get Miss Riley's present ready?" he asked in an anxious tone that reminded her of Anthony's.

"It's in the silver box sitting on the bench in my workroom. Why don't you go get it and when Wendy comes to pick you up, you can take it home, and we'll wrap it together tonight."

"Can I do the bow?"

"Of course."

He dashed off now to the workroom, and Natalie turned to Blanche. "Thanks for going to pick him up. And for this morning." Blanche had come over to Natalie's house and stayed with Kyle until the school bus arrived, while Natalie had raced to the store to meet the first of the deliveries.

Blanche waved Natalie's gratitude aside. "No problem. I enjoy being with Kyle. Besides, my shop isn't as busy as yours this time of year, and I've got good help. I can afford to take a few hours off."

Natalie secretly envied Blanche her full-time clerk. Natalie wished she could afford more help, but some months it was hard enough to make the rent in the pricey Riverwalk location. Blanche never seemed to have that problem.

Sometimes Natalie wondered if the man Blanche was involved with helped her out financially. From some of the presents he'd given her, Natalie assumed he was well-to-do, and from the secretive way Blanche acted— never mentioning his name, never introducing him to her friends—Natalie suspected he was married.

She hoped that wasn't true. Blanche was a good friend, and Natalie didn't want to see her get hurt.

"You saved my life and I owe you, big time. I didn't get a chance to ask you before, but did everything go all right this morning?" Natalie asked.

"Well, actually, we did have to play hide-and-seek with his backpack before the bus came. He hid it last night so robbers couldn't steal it—his words, not mine—then this morning he couldn't remember where he'd put it."

"Where did you finally find it?"

"Kyle's the one who found it, and he wouldn't tell me where because he said it must be a really awesome hiding place if even *he* couldn't find it."

Natalie just shook her head. If there was anything she would change about her son, it was his penchant for hiding things, then forgetting where he'd put them.

Just last week, when Anthony had taken Kyle to his law office one afternoon, Kyle had brought back a state-of-the-art, fancy tape recorder that evidently had fascinated him so much, Anthony had impulsively given it to him. The gift was extravagant and meaningless and much too expensive for a six-year-old, but when Natalie had suggested Kyle should give it back, he'd sworn he couldn't find it. Anywhere.

Natalie sighed. "If I had five bucks for everything that kid has hidden and lost in his short lifetime, I'd be a rich woman."

Blanche laughed, then said in a low voice, "You already were a rich woman. You were married to a Bishop and you gave it all up."

Natalie grimaced. "Don't remind me. Speaking of the devil, he was here today."

Blanche's dark eyebrows rose. "Anthony was here? When?"

"A little while ago. You just missed him. I know you said you were dying to meet him."

"Yes, I am," Blanche said, smiling a little. "What did he want?"

Natalie shrugged. "He said he came to shop for a present for a client's mother."

"That's all he wanted, just to shop?"

Natalie frowned, removing her glasses to polish the lenses with the hem of her sweater. "He did buy something—a music box. Quite an expensive one. But I don't think that's really why he was here. He's up to something, Blanche. I just know it."

"What do you mean?" Blanche rested her forearms on the counter, her dark brown gaze intent.

"He says he wants to do his fatherly duty by Kyle, but I don't buy that. Why now, after all these years?"

Blanche shrugged. "Maybe he feels guilty for his past neglect and wants to make up for it."

Natalie glared at her friend. "You're talking as though he's human. He's not."

Something flashed in Blanche's eyes—something that Natalie couldn't quite discern. "If he's really that bad, why in the world did you ever marry him?"

"You don't know how many times I've asked myself that same question."

"And?"

Natalie hesitated. What was she supposed to say? What excuse could she possibly offer? That she'd been nineteen when she met Anthony? That she'd been working part-time in his law office to help pay her way through college? That her parents were out of the country that year, and she'd been on her own for the first time in her life?

Was she supposed to explain how lonely she'd been? How vulnerable and naive and stupid she'd been? How she'd fallen madly in love with one man and married another? How, by the time she'd turned twenty, she'd been pregnant, miserable, and contemplating divorce?

It was an old story, and a tawdry one. One that didn't bear repeating.

"At least I learned from my mistakes," she finally said. "I'll never trust Anthony Bishop again as long as I live."

"Well," Blanche said carefully. "I guess if the animosity is still that strong between you two, there is another possible reason for Anthony's sudden interest in Kyle."

"What?"

Blanche paused, then shook her dark head and glanced away. "Nothing. It's a crazy idea."

"Nothing concerning Anthony is beyond the realm of possibility," Natalie insisted. "Tell me what you're thinking."

Blanche bit her lip worriedly. "Well, I just wondered. . . . I mean . . . he and his current wife don't have any children, do they?"

"No." A fact that still surprised Natalie. She would have thought Melinda would have tied herself to Anthony in any way she could, but the marriage thus far had remained childless.

"Supposing they can't have children? Supposing Anthony means to go after custody of Kyle?"

Blanche's words hit Natalie like bits of hot shrapnel. Fear exploded inside her. He couldn't. He wouldn't.

But what if—

Suddenly, Anthony's earlier words took on a more sinister meaning.

"He's a Bishop.

Like it or not, Natalie, the boy's my heir.

I'd like him to spend the Christmas holidays with me at Fair Winds.

Supposing you don't have a choice in the matter?"

Anthony had threatened to take Kyle away from her once before, until Natalie had desperately agreed to his terms. She'd held up her end of the bargain all these years, and she'd expected Anthony to do the same.

But maybe that was expecting too much.

She put her hands to the sides of her face. "What if you're right, Blanche? What if he does want custody? He's an attorney. He'd know what to do, who to bribe. The Bishops are so powerful in this city. How would I be able to fight him?" Natalie's tone had risen with each word, until her voice sounded shrill and panicky, even to her own ears.

"Shush. You don't want Kyle to hear you." Blanche reached across the counter and grabbed Natalie's hands, giving them a little shake. "I shouldn't have said anything. It's purely speculation. I had no idea it would upset you this much."

Natalie pulled her hands free from Blanche's and wrapped her arms around her middle. "But it's just like something Anthony would do. He's never forgiven me for leaving like I did. For not taking his guilt money or keeping his name. He thinks I publicly humiliated him. Even after all this time, if he thought he could get back at me by taking Kyle away from me, he'd do it. I know he'd do it."

Anger flickered in Blanche's eyes "But he must really care about his own son—"

"Care? Anthony doesn't know the meaning of the word. None of the Bishops do."

Blanche straightened from her position at the counter, but her gaze was still on Natalie. "I'm sorry. I didn't mean to get you so worked up. I just thought it might be something you ought to consider. You know, forewarned is forearmed."

Natalie began to pace—short, agitated steps that took her to the end of the counter and back. "I won't lose Kyle, Blanche. I can't."

"You're not going to lose Kyle."

"The thought of Anthony raising my son makes my skin crawl."

"It'll never happen," Blanche assured her.

"Damn right, it won't," Natalie said through clenched teeth. "I'll see Anthony Bishop in hell first."

Blanche looked at her in shock. "I've never heard you talk like this."

"You've never seen me threatened." Natalie placed her palms flat on the counter. "I mean it, Blanche. There is no way I would ever let Anthony take Kyle away from me. I don't care what I have to do to stop him."

She was not without a defense, Natalie thought. There was a way to stop Anthony, but before she played that card, she knew she had to be ready to deal with the consequences. Lives would be changed, perhaps forever, and she wasn't at all sure that was a scenario she was ready to face.

Kyle came out of her workroom carrying the silver box that contained the present for his teacher—his light brown, baby-fine hair so like hers and his green eyes so like his father's—and Natalie's throat knotted with emotion. She loved Kyle more than anything, so much so that at times it was a little frightening. If she ever lost him...

You're being ridiculous, she told herself sternly. She was not going to lose Kyle. Not to Anthony or to anyone else.

She and her son were going to have a wonderful Christmas with her parents, who were back in San Antonio now after having lived abroad off and on for the past seven years. And even if the weather was darn near balmy outside, nothing would keep them from getting into the spirit of the season. Christmas had always been Natalie's favorite holiday, and this year would be no exception.

But even as she gave herself a mental pep talk, a sense of unease lingered as she watched her son leave the store with Wendy, his baby-sitter, who had come to pick him up.

What if Blanche was right? What if Anthony was planning to take Kyle away from her?

Chapter Two

Anthony Bishop stood at the floor-to-ceiling windows in his law office and stared out at the ever-changing skyline of the Alamo city. San Antonio, now the ninth-largest city in the country, was growing by leaps and bounds, and it excited Anthony no end to know that he was as much a part of the city's future as his father, grandfather and great-grandfather had been of its past.

Single-handedly, Anthony had guided Bishop, Bishop, and Winslow—once a small, but extremely prestigious law practice—toward the twenty-first century, expanding and diversifying until the firm now boasted more than fifty partners and associates. And he had been able to do so in the amazingly short period of time since his father had died because Anthony wasn't afraid of taking a few chances. He wasn't afraid to gamble now and then. What was life without risk?

Truth be told, he liked living on the edge. He liked flirting with disaster, and he always, *always* loved to win.

Anthony thought about his latest coup as his gaze scanned the horizon. Darkness had fallen and he could see the lights twinkling on the Tower of the Americas, built for the 1968 World's Fair, and farther east, the newer, but no less impressive architectural wonder called the Alamodome.

Partially obscured by towering office buildings, a ribbon of light festooned the heart of downtown known as the Riverwalk—a shimmering collage of restaurants and specialty shops built along the banks of the San Antonio River.

Anthony stared at the spot where Natalie's store was located. Who would have thought that little venture— a Christmas specialty shop open the year around— would have turned out so successfully?

Certainly not him, Anthony had to admit. That was one gamble that hadn't paid off. When Natalie had opened Silver Bells five years ago, a year after the divorce, he'd been sure she would fall flat on her face and come crying back to him, begging for a second chance.

But Natalie Silver never begged for anything. She was too proud. Too stubborn. She hadn't asked for a cent of his money when they'd split up, and had only grudgingly accepted the child support Anthony had instructed his attorney to offer. She hadn't taken anything but Kyle when she'd moved out. Hadn't even kept the Bishop name, damn her. Damn her all to hell.

But in the next instant he was telling himself, *It's not too late. You can win her back if you want her.*

He'd won her once from his own brother. He could do so again, if he chose to. After all, everyone had a price. Even Natalie.

"Mr. Bishop?"

He whirled at the sound of his secretary's voice. "What is it?"

"Your wife called earlier while you were out. I told her you were in a meeting and couldn't be disturbed. Was that all right?"

"Exactly right." The last person he wanted to talk to tonight was that shrew who passed herself off as his loving wife.

He walked over and sat down at his desk, running his finger down the neat list of the next day's appointments.

"Did you get the McGruder meeting rescheduled?" he asked abruptly.

"Yes. He's coming in next week." The secretary wavered in the doorway.

Anthony glanced up, scowling. "Well?"

"Will you be needing anything else tonight?" she asked hesitantly, as if dreading to hear his answer.

Anthony glanced at his Rolex. It was after eight. He supposed the woman was anxious to get home to her family—did she even have a family?—or perhaps meet a boyfriend for drinks or some Christmas shopping. Later, they would probably go back to her place or to his and . . .

Anthony's thoughts trailed off as he let his eyes linger on the woman's legs. She really was very attractive. Why hadn't he noticed her before?

She cleared her throat, blushing prettily as she became aware of his attention. "If there's nothing else . . ."

Anthony sighed with regret. Another night, perhaps. He had too many things on his mind right now to pursue the subtle art of seduction, and besides, he already had too many entanglements, both personal and professional, from which he needed to extricate himself. Speaking of which—"Is my sister still here?"

"She's in her office. Shall I get her for you?"

"No, no." Absently he waved the secretary away. If his wife was the last person he wanted to see tonight, his sister was a close second. Anthea was getting just a little too ambitious for her own good. And a little too clever. She'd been asking him a lot of questions about the Russo case, as if she suspected something. As if she *knew* something.

In spite of the bond Anthony shared with his twin sister, he knew the time was fast approaching when he would have to do something about her. But like Melinda, his current wife, she would have to be handled carefully. Neither of them would go quietly.

And, of course, there was the matter of his mistress to contend with; a woman of unparalleled talents and tastes, to be sure, but lately she'd become possessive, clinging. Desperate. And she'd been making threats. Nothing to be concerned about, of course, but still, after their interlude here a little while ago, she'd left in tears, begging him not to send her away. Begging him for more than he was willing to give. Anthony had known then that something would have to be done, and soon.

A clean break from all of them was exactly what he needed right now. Maybe then . . .

He stared at the picture of Kyle on the corner of his desk. It was time for the boy to come home. Preferably with his mother, but if that wasn't possible—

The phone on Anthony's desk rang, and he noticed it was his private line. Only a handful of people had access to that number, his wife not among them. Warily, he picked up the phone and said hello.

A gruff voice he recognized instantly said, "It's me. Is the line clear?"

"It's clear." Anthony routinely had his office and phone lines swept for electronic bugs, but since Jack Russo had gotten out of prison a few days ago, Anthony had to be twice as careful. He knew the feds were watching him closely, and he couldn't afford to let his guard down even for a second.

Of course, there were ways around the surveillance, he thought, smiling. Ways of slipping in and out of his office without anyone—even his secretary—being the wiser.

From the other end came a long hesitation, then Russo said, "I received your package."

"And?"

"And? *And?*" Russo screamed. "There was nothing inside that box but a goddamned ceramic Santa Claus thing."

"What? That's impossible—"

"What the hell's going on here, Bishop? Where the hell are my diamonds?"

Anthony swallowed, tasting bile. What the hell *was* going on? "Look, Jack, just calm down. The diamonds have to be in that package. All of them, except for my cut. I put them inside the music box. There's a catch on the back that opens a secret compartment—"

"I've smashed it to bits and I'm telling you, those diamonds are not here. Now you better come clean with me, Bishop. I didn't rot in no stinking federal pen for two and a half years to be double-crossed by my own attorney."

Anthony felt as if a noose were slowly tightening around his neck. He reached up and loosened his tie. "I'm telling you, I put them in there myself. Someone on your end—"

"There's no one here but me and my mother," Russo growled. "And I sure as hell didn't give myself the shaft. If you're implying that my mother—"

"No, no. I didn't mean that," Anthony said quickly, remembering the devotion Russo felt for his elderly mother.

"Well, then. That just leaves you now, don't it?"

Anthony's mind raced. What the hell had happened? Was it possible? Could Natalie have found the diamonds and removed them? He might expect a double cross like that from Melinda, but Natalie?

"Those diamonds are the only thing tying me to that murder, Bishop. If I go down, you go down."

"No one's going down," Anthony said hastily, running his fingers through his hair. "This is some kind of mistake."

"Damn right, it's a mistake. *Your* mistake, buddy, and you better, by God, fix it. You've got twenty-four hours before my boys come calling."

Anthony closed his eyes briefly as an image of Russo's thugs sprang to mind. "Trust me," he said. "Haven't I always taken care of you? Didn't I get the murder charges thrown out for lack of evidence?"

"Yeah, but if those sparklers turn up in the wrong hands—"

"They won't," Anthony assured him. The diamonds had to be still in Natalie's store. Somehow the wrong music box must have been sent. Whether deliberately or by mistake, Anthony had no idea, but he was damned well going to find out. "I'll go over to my ex-wife's shop tonight after she closes. I'll search every inch of that damned store until I find those diamonds."

"You better hope to hell she didn't rat you out," Russo said ominously. "It'll be your hide I come looking for."

Anthony got the message loud and clear. He stared at the silent phone for a moment, then hung up the receiver with trembling hands.

Outside his office, a soft rustling sound startled him. Silently, he got up and strode across the carpeted floor to his door. He pulled it open and gazed around his secretary's office.

No one was about. The desk was tidied for the night, the computer turned off, the files all locked away. But the door that led into the hallway was slightly ajar, and from outside the office came the unmistakable hum of the elevator, as someone made an exit.

"DAMN, DAMN, DOUBLE DAMN," Natalie muttered as she gazed at the glowing red light on her security system in Silver Bells. She'd been in such a hurry to close up shop and get home, that she must have forgotten to turn on the alarm.

She sighed wearily. It was after eleven and she was exhausted. Normally she closed the shop at six, but during the Christmas season, she stayed open until nine. Tonight she hadn't gotten rid of the last customer until almost ten, and then she'd had to close out the register and tidy the shop before locking up.

She'd made it almost all the way home before remembering that she hadn't put her bank bag in the safe before leaving. She'd tried to convince herself that the bag would be perfectly safe in her desk drawer until morning. She'd never had a break-in, and the Riverwalk was well patrolled, especially this time of year. But a little voice in the back of her mind kept warning: *There's always a first time for everything.*

Natalie had known that niggling little voice wouldn't give her a moment's peace until she drove back to the shop and locked the bank bag in her safe. And now, as she gazed at the mocking red light, she decided it was a good thing she had.

The overhead lights were off, but the Christmas lights were still on, illuminating the interior of Silver Bells with a soft, sterling glow. Natalie stopped, her breath catching slightly at the beauty, at the magic of the moment.

She had done this, she thought, gazing around in wonder. She had done this all on her own. She'd made a success of her shop, made her dream come true, and although she didn't expect to ever be rich, at least she and Kyle would be comfortable.

That was important to her; being able to provide for her son without any help from the Bishops. Because if Natalie had learned anything during her short marriage to Anthony, it was that the Bishops never gave anything without demanding something in return.

Without turning on the overhead lights, Natalie made her way around the counter and headed for the workroom when suddenly she came to a full stop. The door to the workroom was open, and Natalie always kept it closed. Something—a subtle sound, a current of displaced air, a scent?—warned her that she wasn't alone. Someone was inside the darkened workroom, listening to the silence just as she was.

How had the intruder gotten in? The front door had been locked. There was no sign of a forced entry, but the alarm had been turned off. Maybe she hadn't forgotten to turn it on after all. Maybe the intruder had managed to pick the lock neatly and disarm her security system, which meant she was dealing with a professional. Someone as dangerous as he was experienced.

Natalie's heart hammered in her chest. What should she do? Turn and make a run for it? Find a weapon? What? *What?*

For a split second, fear paralyzed her and she stood rooted to the spot, listening to the sound of her own blood pounding in her ears. Then, before she had time to regain her senses, the intruder stepped out of the workroom to confront her in the cool glow of Christmas lights.

"Where are they?" he demanded.

Natalie stared at Anthony in shock. "What are you doing here?" she finally managed to gasp. "How did you get in?"

He grabbed her arm and pulled her roughly into the workroom. For the first time in her life, Natalie was actually frightened of her ex-husband. She'd never seen him look so dangerous. So out of control.

She gazed around at the wreckage that was her workroom. Drawers were pulled out of her desk, the contents dumped on the floor. The shelves against the wall had been ruthlessly cleared, and even the garbage can had been overturned.

Anger warred with fear. Natalie jerked her arm from his grasp and whirled to face him. "What the hell do you think you're doing?"

His green gaze, usually so cool, flashed with fire. "Where are they, Natalie?"

"I don't know what you're talking about, but I'm calling the police. Even you can't get away with this, Anthony." She started toward the phone on her desk, but he reached it first, grabbed it, and ripped it from the jack.

"You found them, didn't you?" He threw the phone against the wall, shattering the plastic housing. "You thought you could pull a fast one on me, didn't you? You've always been just a little too clever for your own good, Natalie. But not this time. Now hand them over before I do something we might both regret—''

The door to the shop was behind Natalie, and Anthony's gaze moved over her right shoulder. His eyes widened in surprise. ''What are you doing he—''

Before Natalie could turn, something hit her on the back of the head, sending sharp, shooting pains through her skull. Stunned, she felt her knees buckle and she collapsed to the floor.

Chapter Three

Anthony Bishop had been dead for hours, and his brother still found it hard to believe. As Spence stared at the police report, the words blurred before his eyes. It didn't matter. He'd read it so many times since Anthony's body had been found that he knew the words by heart, anyway.

Anthony had been stabbed in the back with a long, serrated knife that Natalie Silver kept in her workroom to open shipping cartons. When the police had answered a disturbance call at her shop just after midnight last night, they'd found Natalie kneeling over Anthony, clutching the bloody weapon in her hand.

But perhaps the most compelling evidence of all was Anthony's own words, spoken just seconds before he died. "Natalie...not you..."

It had been nearly twelve hours since Spence had learned of his brother's murder. He'd only left police headquarters once, very briefly, to break the news to his mother and sister, who hadn't even known Spence was in town.

His return to San Antonio had been masked in secrecy, cloaked in subterfuge, and now it had all blown up in his face.

He rubbed his eyes, wondering how the hell it had come to this. His assignment had been to bring down Jack Russo by finding the diamonds that would tie the mobster to a brutal murder in Dallas three years ago— before Russo had been sent to prison on racketeering charges.

Spence had known all along that in bringing down Russo there was a good chance Anthony would be implicated; that his brother might have to face criminal charges if the FBI's suspicions about him proved true.

But that fact hadn't deterred Spence. He'd been willing to do whatever it took to get Jack Russo—even sacrifice his own brother—because he'd convinced himself over the years that the end justified the means.

Now Anthony was dead and Natalie Silver was accused of his murder. Spence wished he could appreciate the irony of the situation, but he couldn't. He felt empty inside. Hollow in the place where his grief should have been. No matter what Anthony had done, he hadn't deserved this.

And Natalie?

Did she deserve the hell she was being put through?

Spence closed his eyes, telling himself that if she had done this to his brother, he wouldn't lift one finger to help her.

But he would.

He knew he would, because his gut instinct told him that she was as much a part of his assignment as Anthony had been. She held the key, and if he wanted to win, if he wanted to crack this case, Spence would have to keep his eye—a close eye—on Natalie Silver.

Jack Russo was a cold-blooded murderer, and Spence knew he would do whatever it took to bring him to justice. Even if it meant helping a woman who had once betrayed him.

Or bringing her down.

THIS WAS A NIGHTMARE, Natalie thought, as she gazed at the stony-eyed detectives intent on interrogating her again. She'd answered so many questions, told her story so many times since last night, she felt numb with exhaustion. She could almost understand how a suspect could be coerced into a confession. Just say yes, and maybe they would leave you alone; give you a moment's peace.

But Natalie had a feeling that for her, peace would be a long time in coming.

The worst part was she hadn't been able to see Kyle. She hadn't been the one to tell him Anthony was dead. Instead, after her desperate phone call from police headquarters last night, Natalie's parents had rushed over to her house, relieved the baby-sitter—who had been frantic with worry by that time—and when Kyle had awakened this morning, they'd told him what had happened as gently as possible, leaving out the gruesome aspects of Anthony's death and the fact that Natalie had been arrested for his murder.

Oh, God, if only she could remember, Natalie thought desperately. If only she could recall what had happened before she'd blacked out. Someone had come in, hit her on the head, then killed Anthony while she was still unconscious. But who? Who would do such a terrible thing and leave her to take the blame?

"If you didn't stab him, why were you holding the murder weapon when the officers arrived on the scene?" one of the detectives, a Sergeant Phillips, asked her.

Natalie stared at him, bleary-eyed. "I told you. I didn't even realize I was holding it. I don't even know how the knife got in my hand. When I regained consciousness, I saw Anthony on the floor. There was so much blood...I knelt over him to see if he was still alive, and that's when the police came storming in."

"How do you explain that cut on your right hand?" the other detective asked.

"I...I can't explain it," Natalie said, moistening her dry lips. She hadn't even realized she was cut until the officers who arrived on the scene wrapped a bandage around it to stop the bleeding.

Sergeant Phillips propped one foot on a chair and folded his arms across his bent knee. "Your divorce from Anthony Bishop was pretty nasty, wasn't it? Accusations all around. Rumors and innuendos flying. You didn't get a settlement from that divorce, did you?"

"No."

"You must have thought you were entitled to one."

"I didn't want one. I didn't want anything from Anthony except my freedom. And my son."

Sergeant Phillips arched an eyebrow at that. He and the other detective exchanged glances. Then Phillips said, "Anthony Bishop married his current wife just three weeks after his divorce from you became final, isn't that so?"

Natalie nodded.

"Her name was Seagrass before she became a Bishop. Melinda Seagrass. The two of you were once close. You went to school together. In fact, she was your best friend, wasn't she?"

"Yes."

"Married her just three weeks after he divorced you." Sergeant Phillips stared at her. "It's a pretty safe bet the two of them were seeing each other before the divorce. Wouldn't you say so?"

Natalie sighed. "I know what you're getting at. But I didn't carry a grudge against Anthony because of his affair with Melinda. That happened years ago. I didn't kill him for revenge, if that's what you're thinking."

"Then why did you kill him?"

"I didn't!" Dear God, she had to make them believe her. Why wouldn't they listen to her? She pushed back her hair with both hands. "I told you, I walked in on Anthony at the shop last night. I have no idea what he was doing there, but evidently he was looking for something. He thought I had something of his. But before he could tell me what it was, someone else came in and hit me from behind. I lost consciousness. When I woke up, I saw Anthony lying on the floor... covered in blood..." She closed her eyes, trying to maintain her composure. "I swear that's all I know," she said through trembling lips.

"If he was already inside the shop when you got there, how did he get in? There was no sign of a forced entry, and the security system had been turned off. How do you explain that?"

"I ... don't know. I might have forgotten to turn the alarm on when I left earlier."

"Did you also forget to lock the front door?"

"No..."

Sergeant Phillips got up from the chair and walked around the table to sit directly across from Natalie. His dark eyes bored into hers so intently that she even began to feel guilty. She clasped her hands in her lap to try and control the shaking. "Did you know that your ex-husband was about to haul you into court and sue you for sole custody of your son?''

Natalie gasped. ''No—''

''The papers were already drawn up. Are you telling me you had no idea of his intentions? Not even an inkling?''

Natalie hesitated, remembering her conversation yesterday with Blanche. They'd talked about the possibility then, and Natalie had said something like— Dear God—she'd said if Anthony were to try to take away her son, she would do whatever it took to stop him. But she hadn't meant it! She hadn't meant she would kill him!

''You did know, didn't you?''

Natalie shook her head. ''No. I mean ... I wondered why he'd suddenly come back into our lives, why he wanted to start seeing Kyle again. But I didn't know he planned to sue for custody. He never said anything.''

''He never threatened you?''

''No.''

''You didn't call him down to your shop last night to confront him with your suspicions?''

''No.''

''He didn't taunt you with how easy it would be for a high-powered attorney like him, a *Bishop,* to win in court? To take your son away from you?''

''No.''

''The two of you didn't fight? He didn't get physical? Shove you around? You didn't take that knife out of your desk, catch him off guard, and stab him in the back?''

''No! No!'' Natalie screamed, jumping to her feet. ''I was knocked unconscious, just like I've told you a million times. I have a bump on my head to prove it.''

"Sit down," Sergeant Phillips instructed calmly. When she complied, he said, "You could have gotten that during the struggle."

"I didn't," Natalie cried. "And I didn't kill Anthony!" She dropped her head in her hands. "Oh, God, why won't you believe me?"

"I'm not unsympathetic to your predicament," Sergeant Phillips said in a deceptively soft voice. Natalie looked up, wanting to believe that note of kindness, that hint of empathy in his dark eyes. "You love your son very much, don't you?"

Natalie swallowed and nodded.

"A boy needs his mother."

Tears flooded Natalie's eyes as she thought about Kyle. How had he taken the news of Anthony's death? Was he sad, grieving? Until a few weeks ago, Kyle hadn't seen Anthony since he was a baby. He didn't know him. But still, Natalie knew her son had thought about him over the years, wondered about him. Kyle must be so upset, so confused. And she wasn't there for him.

"You would do anything to protect him, wouldn't you?"

Natalie looked up through teary eyes but she said nothing.

"He needs you now more than ever. And you need to be with him. Cooperate with me, Natalie, and I'll see that you and your son are together again very soon."

"What do I have to do?" she asked weakly.

"Just tell me the truth." Sergeant Phillips leaned forward, gazing earnestly into her eyes. "You see, I think you killed Anthony Bishop in self-defense. I think what we have here is a case of justifiable homicide. Just admit it, and the chances are, you'll walk out of here a free woman.''

SILENCE FELL LIKE A heavy cloak over the interrogation room. Everyone seemed to be waiting with bated breath for Natalie's answer. She sat stone still, gazing at the sergeant with the most haunted-looking eyes Spence had ever seen.

He found himself leaning toward the two-way mirror, his gaze searching her face for the truth. But he hadn't seen Natalie Silver in seven years. He wasn't sure he would recognize the truth in her eyes if he saw it.

Seven years, he thought. Seven years since he had returned to San Antonio following his first big undercover assignment, only to find that she had married his brother while he'd been gone. She'd wasted no time in discovering who had the money in his family. Who had the power.

Natalie Silver had fooled him once with her sweet smile and innocent eyes, but Spence didn't think she was capable of doing so again. He wasn't a rookie anymore. During the years he'd been an agent, he'd dealt with plenty of liars. And murderers.

He studied her features now, looking for the telltale clues that would give her away, surprised to find that his memories of her were amazingly accurate. Her light brown hair was longer now, shoulder length and cut in layers that fell softly around her face. She wore a dark red sweater and a short plaid skirt that made her seem very young, almost schoolgirlish. And vulnerable. Still vulnerable.

She wasn't wearing her glasses, and Spence wanted to believe that was why her blue eyes looked so lost. So haunted.

Or maybe it was because of what she'd done, he told himself grimly.

As if she sensed his anger, Natalie's gaze shifted from Sergeant Phillips and for one split second, she seemed to be gazing at the blind side of the mirror, staring through the glass directly into Spence's soul. The sensation startled him, and before he realized what he was doing, he took a step back, as if protecting himself from her.

Then her gaze refocused on Phillips and she said in a soft, quivering voice, "I want to see my son. More than anything."

"Of course, you do. We want that, too." The two detectives exchanged triumphant looks. They were working her well. Had her right where they wanted her. Exhaustion and fear had worn her down, stripped away her defenses, and now they were playing on her emotions. Making her think they had only her best interests at heart before they zeroed in for the kill.

In their place, Spence would have done exactly the same thing.

"Tell us what really happened, Natalie," Sergeant Phillips urged softly. "We only want to help you."

Natalie closed her eyes for a moment, as if gathering her courage. Spence felt the muscles in the back of his neck tighten in anticipation. He found himself straining toward the speaker.

When she opened her eyes, they seemed even bluer than before. And clearer somehow. "I...can't lie to get out of here. I can't tell you something that isn't true. I didn't kill Anthony. Not in self-defense or for any other reason."

Anger flashed across Sergeant Phillips's usually stoic features. "The evidence says otherwise."

"I didn't do it," Natalie repeated.

"Then my best advice to you," Phillips said, rising, "is to get your lawyer down here, pronto. You're in a lot of trouble, lady."

NATALIE SAT AT THE wooden table, staring down at her bandaged hand. Funny, she couldn't feel the cut beneath the gauze. Not even so much as a sting, and yet she knew the cut was fairly deep. Before bringing her to police headquarters last night, the officers had taken her to the emergency room at one of the local hospitals for stitches.

Natalie had no idea how she'd gotten that cut. Or if the dark stains across the front of her skirt and sweater were her blood or...Anthony's.

The detectives—Sergeant Phillips and the other one— had left her alone several minutes ago, probably to let her contemplate her predicament before they came back in for another round of questions. She was sure this was one of their tactics. Attack and retreat, attack and retreat, so that the waiting between rounds became unbearable.

Natalie wasn't sure how much more she could take. Her father had advised her this morning to say nothing until he could find her a good attorney, but Natalie had been so sure that once she told her story to the police, everything would be okay; she would be released. All she had to do was tell the truth, and she would be set free.

But that hadn't been the case at all. No one believed her. Everyone seemed convinced of her guilt. Dear God, what was she going to do?

She rested her head in her hands, tempted to give in to despair. But she had to think about Kyle. She had to be strong for him. She had to get out of here so she could take care of her son.

Even though she had been expecting it, when the door opened a few minutes later, Natalie jumped. She swung her gaze around, determined to face the next round of interrogation bravely, but the moment she saw the man in the doorway, her courage all but deserted her.

For the space of a heartbeat, she thought she might be seeing things. Thought he might be a mirage. Spencer Bishop was the last person on earth she'd expected to see.

Or wanted to see.

Their gazes held for the longest moment, then Spence slowly closed the door behind him. Natalie had never felt so defenseless. She sat huddled at the table, shivering beneath the piercing glare of his cold, green eyes.

Bishop eyes.

"What are you doing here?" she finally managed.

The expression on his face never wavered. He walked to the table and stood over her, tall, dark, and dangerously handsome. "I would have thought that obvious."

She gazed up at him, the very sight of him—the memories of him—making her tremble. "I didn't do it," she whispered. "I didn't kill Anthony."

He didn't say anything, merely studied her for a moment longer, then said, "I should advise you that you don't have to talk to me. You don't have to talk to any of us without an attorney present. They told you that, didn't they? They advised you of your rights?"

"Yes. But I don't have an attorney."

"Then you'd better get one."

"But I'm innocent!"

Spence shrugged. "It's in your best interests to have someone here advising you. Anything you say can and will be used against you."

"Then you're here in an official capacity?" she asked.

His gazed darkened on her. "I'm here because my brother is dead."

"And you think I killed him, just like the police do." The irony of the situation was devastating. Natalie didn't know which was worse—facing a steely-eyed FBI agent or the accusing eyes of the man she had once loved.

Spence sat down at the table across from her. Natalie tried not to look up, but his gaze was too penetrating, his presence too compelling. She glanced up, searching his face for a sign of the man she'd once loved.

But then, that man hadn't really existed, had he? Just like Anthony, he'd made her believe what she'd wanted to believe. Until he'd gotten what he wanted.

Natalie's faced burned with humiliation. Even after seven years, the thought that she had been little more than a one-night stand to Spencer Bishop still shamed her. How could she have been so stupid, falling for a man she'd known less than a week? The dashing young FBI agent, so dark and intense...

He hadn't changed that much, she thought weakly. A little older, maybe. A little harder. He was wearing jeans, snug and riding low on his lean frame, and a dark shirt, dark tie, and sports coat. Natalie wondered where his gun was.

His green eyes narrowed on her, as if reading her thoughts. He reached up and drew his fingers through his dark hair, making Natalie remember yet another intimacy.

"The evidence is pretty damning," Spence said. "Especially Anthony's last words. What do you think he meant if he wasn't pointing the finger at you? 'Natalie...not you...' Those were his exact words, I believe."

"I know. I was there." Her eyes filled with tears as she remembered those last few moments of Anthony's life, when she had awakened to see him lying on the floor, so still and covered with blood. She'd knelt over him, unaware of picking up the murder weapon, intent only on finding out if he was still alive, if she could help him.

And then the police had burst through the front door. The lights had come on, and Natalie had looked up to find the officers' guns drawn on her. "Move away from the body. Now!" And another one shouting, "Drop your weapon!"

Dazed, Natalie had complied. While one of the officers had stood guard over her, the other had rushed to Anthony's side to try and stanch the flow of blood. But it had been too late. Too late for anything other than Anthony's last dying words.

Natalie...not you...

Natalie had no idea why her ex-husband had said what he'd said, but the thought had crossed her mind that perhaps he had deliberately tried to implicate her. But why, unless he hadn't known he was mortally wounded? Unless he'd thought, even on his deathbed, that he could somehow use his attack against her? If he hadn't known he was dying, he might still have been thinking of his custody suit. What better way to get Kyle than by sending his mother to prison?

But Anthony had died, and Natalie was accused of his murder. Where did that leave Kyle now? Surely Irene wouldn't go after custody. She'd never shown the slightest interest in her grandson. But what if...

Another possibility occurred to her, and a cold chill swept through her as she stared at Spence. Things had changed since Anthony's death. Natalie was not only fighting for her own life, she was fighting for her son's life, as well.

Spence was still looking at her, as if he could read her every thought. Shaken, Natalie glanced away. "I won't say another word," she said, "until I get an attorney."

"Suit yourself." He got up, but leaned toward her over the table, invading her space. She could smell the subtle scent of his cologne, see the faint shadow of his beard. The effect was powerful. Natalie's pulse hammered in her throat. She had to fight the urge to back away from him, to protect herself from the memories his presence stirred to life.

Then he straightened and strode across the room to the door, glancing back over his shoulder. "Believe it or not, I'm not after you, Natalie. I'm after the truth."

"I wish I could believe that," she whispered as the door closed between them.

Chapter Four

Daylight had come and gone, and twilight fell softly on the city as Natalie prepared to spend her first full night in jail. She gazed around her dismal surroundings—the grim tile floor, the cinder-block walls, the sink and toilet, and the two cots, one of them occupied by her only cell mate, a woman named Jessie who had slept almost the whole time since Natalie had been back from the bail-review hearing.

She wished the woman would wake up and talk to her, and then again, she didn't. She'd seen movies about innocent people being locked up with hardened criminals, and she had no idea what Jessie was in for.

And then the shocking thought occurred to Natalie that perhaps the woman was only pretending to sleep. Maybe she was the one who was scared. Scared to be incarcerated with a murderer.

Natalie sat down on the other cot and shivered. She'd already been branded a killer. It didn't matter that she was innocent. The police thought she was guilty, and so would everyone else when they heard the evidence. Maybe even the jury.

Natalie wrapped her arms around herself as her shivering grew worse. What if she was convicted? What if

she was sent to prison for the rest of her life? What if
the only time she got to see Kyle or her parents was on
visitors' day, and even then through a sheet of bullet-
proof glass?

She squeezed her eyes closed as she rocked back and
forth, not wanting to cry. Not wanting to give in to the
despair, because if she did, she knew she would be lost.

But it was difficult to hold on to her courage when
everything seemed so hopeless. With the police so convinced of her guilt, they wouldn't be looking for any
other suspects. And bail had been set so high—a quarter of a million dollars—that Natalie wouldn't be able
to get out of here to search for the real killer herself.

That had been the Bishops' doing, Natalie thought
bitterly. Having bail set so high that she couldn't possibly make it, not even if she sold her house, her shop,
and cleaned out her savings account. Irene Bishop had
obviously called in her markers, and Natalie would have
to remain in jail, possibly until the trial, which could be
weeks or even months away. The loss of Christmas sales
would force her out of business. She would lose everything.

But worst of all, she wouldn't be able to be with Kyle,
to protect him and shelter him from the nightmare their
lives had suddenly become.

"Natalie Silver?"

She looked up to find a female police officer opening the cell door.

"Ye-yes." Natalie rose.

"Come with me," the officer said. "Your bail's been
posted. You're free to go."

Natalie stared at the woman in shock. "But how?
Who?"

The officer shrugged. "He's downstairs now, filling out the paperwork. Come on. You want to get out of here, don't you?"

Natalie had never wanted anything so badly in her life. She didn't know how her father had managed to come up with the money in so short a time, but she was thankful that he had.

As she walked through the cell door, she glanced back. Her cell mate had rolled over and was staring at her with the most haunted eyes Natalie had ever seen, and it occurred to her that looking at Jessie was like looking into a mirror.

"OPEN IT UP," the officer instructed as she shoved a manila envelope toward Natalie. "Make sure everything's there."

Natalie did as she was told, but if anything was missing, she wouldn't know it. She couldn't remember what personal effects had been taken from her last night.

"Where's my father?" she asked, signing for the articles.

The officer shrugged. "How should I know?"

Natalie glanced up. "He's the one who posted bail for me, isn't he?"

She pointed past Natalie's right shoulder. "That's him over there."

Natalie turned around, clutching the manila envelope to her breast. Spencer Bishop stood in the doorway of an office, talking to someone. He hadn't seen her yet, and Natalie started to back away. But then he turned, and his gaze, like the touch of a chill wind, fell on her.

Slowly he left the doorway and walked toward her. Natalie's heart beat like a tom-tom as he stopped in front of her and stared down into her upturned face.

In the years since she'd seen him, Natalie had managed to forget—or at least she told herself she had—how tall he was, how broad his shoulders were. How masculine he could seem with the five o'clock shadow that never quite went away. His green eyes looked darker and deeper than she remembered, almost sinister as he held her gaze without wavering.

"Why?" she whispered, not trusting herself to say much else.

He merely stared at her for a moment longer, then shrugged. "I figured you were ready to get out of that place. Was I wrong?"

Natalie shook her head. God, no, he wasn't wrong. If there was one thing she'd discovered during this whole ordeal, it was that a jail cell was the loneliest place in the world. The thought of spending the night in there—of spending a *lifetime* of nights in there—sent a shiver of dread coursing through Natalie.

"You're not wrong," she said softly. "But I don't understand why you did it. Your family—"

"Let's leave my family out of it, shall we?"

"I just don't understand why you would do this for me."

"Unless I want something in return?" he asked, his voice edged with sarcasm.

Natalie glanced away. That was exactly what she was thinking.

"Well, you're right," he said. "I do want something from you."

"What?" she asked, although she was almost afraid to hear his answer. He was a Bishop, after all.

"I want to find out the truth," he said. "I want to know why Anthony was murdered. You're the only one who can help me find the answers I need."

She took a deep breath, staring up at him, not trusting him. "Does this mean you think I'm innocent?"

"In the eyes of the law, you're innocent until proven guilty."

"That doesn't really answer my question," she said.

"It's the best I can give you right now."

"Then I guess it'll have to do," she said quietly. Lifting her chin, Natalie met his gaze evenly, until, this time, it was Spence who glanced away. "Thank you for getting me out of here," she said, even though she still didn't understand why he had. She didn't know anything. If Spence was looking for answers from her, he was going to be sadly disappointed.

"I didn't do it for thanks," he said. "Like I said, I want to find out the truth. And having you free makes that a whole lot easier for me."

"How?"

He hesitated, as if contemplating how much to tell her. "We can work together. You must want those answers as badly as I do."

"But I don't know anything," she said. "I've told the police everything. What more can I do?"

"Something may come back to you," he said. "And if it does, I want to be the first to know."

"By bailing me out of jail, you think you've bought my cooperation. Is that it?" she asked bitterly.

He shrugged. "Maybe. Like it or not, Natalie, I'm all you've got right now." His eyes grew even darker, deeper, until Natalie felt as though she were drowning in those green depths. As if suddenly, unexpectedly, she was once again over her head in dangerous waters.

She shivered, wishing she could trust Spence's motives. But he'd lied to her before. Deceived her just as cruelly as Anthony had. Natalie didn't trust any of the Bishops and she knew she never would.

"If you'll excuse me, I need to call a cab," she said, turning away.

"I'll drive you home."

That stopped her. She turned back, staring at him suspiciously. "Why? So you can grill me on the way?"

"I was just leaving, and this time of night, cabs are hard to come by. No ulterior motive," he said, holding up his hands.

And what did it matter if he did have an ulterior motive? Natalie decided. She wasn't going to tell him anything, and besides, ulterior motives could work both ways. Maybe she could do a little grilling of her own, find out the real reason he'd posted her bail. Because she knew, intuitively, that he wasn't telling her the whole truth.

"In that case, I accept," she said, praying she didn't live to regret this night. "Thank you, again."

"No problem."

It took them twenty minutes to get to Natalie's parents' house in Alamo Heights. Twenty excruciatingly silent minutes, during which time both of them seemed equally determined not to tell the other one anything. When Spence pulled into the driveway, Natalie's eyes filled with sudden tears.

Christmas lights outlined the curves and gables of the roof and every window and doorway of the modest-but-comfortable house. A wreath hung on the front door and a big red bow adorned the mailbox.

Had there ever been a more welcome sight? Natalie thought fleetingly.

But as Spence got out of the car and followed her up the drive, she hesitated. They stood at the bottom of the porch steps, suspended in the warm glow of Christmas lights, as she gazed with trepidation at the front door.

"What's the matter?" he asked. "I thought you would be anxious to get home."

"I am." Natalie took a deep breath. The whole thing was just too much, she thought. She'd been accused of murdering her ex-husband, while here she stood with his brother in her parents' front yard. Could her life get any more bizarre?

"It's just... What if I look into their eyes and see that they don't believe me? What if my own son thinks I'm a murderer?"

In the glow of the Christmas lights, she saw a shadow crossing his features, and Natalie had a sudden premonition of what he was thinking. If the situation were reversed, it wouldn't matter much whether his family believed in his innocence or not. They would condemn him for dragging the Bishop name through the mud.

"Well, there's only one way to find out," he said, his voice hard.

Natalie nodded, but before she could say anything, the front door swung open and a deep voice said excitedly, "Natalie! I thought that was you! Come here, sweetheart!"

And suddenly Natalie knew everything was going to be all right. The tears that she'd managed to hold at bay for so long came flooding out at the sight of her father's outstretched arms. She flew up the steps and into that waiting comfort.

"Daddy," she whispered, squeezing her eyes tightly shut against the rush of emotions brought on by the warmth and security of Paul Silver's embrace. The scent of Old Spice had always reminded her of her father, but never had it smelled more wonderful, conjured more memories, than it did at that moment.

"I know," he said, holding her tightly. "I know, sweetheart, but everything's going to be okay now. You'll see."

He whispered to her and soothed her just as he had when she was a little girl, when she'd come to him with nothing more traumatic than a skinned knee or a broken doll. He was not a big man—only five foot seven or so—and he was still recovering from a heart attack he'd suffered two months ago. But Natalie thought his arms had never felt stronger.

Presently they both became aware of Spence, standing at the bottom of the steps, and her father cleared his throat gruffly. "Why don't you both come in and tell me how you got out. I've had our lawyer and accountant working non-stop since the hearing this afternoon, but I didn't have any hope of getting anything done until morning."

Natalie hesitated, realizing her father had just invited Spencer Bishop into his home, and neither she nor Spence seemed to know what to do about the request.

"I can't stay," he said.

At the same time, she said, "It's okay. Please come in."

Spence hesitated, as if staying here was the last thing in the world he wanted to do at that moment. But then he shrugged, and climbed the porch steps to follow them inside.

The interior of the house was even more welcoming. Boughs of fresh fir and holly, draping the banister and mantel, perfumed the air, and a cheery fire crackled in the fireplace. A huge Christmas tree, decorated with colored lights and a myriad of ornaments in every conceivable shape and size, dominated one whole corner of the living room.

The fire must have been her mother's idea, Natalie thought. Joy Silver always said there was nothing quite so comforting as a fire on a winter evening—even if, in San Antonio, it often meant running the air conditioner at the same time.

Her father kept his left arm around Natalie's shoulders as he turned to Spence. For the first time, Natalie realized there was more gray than brown in her father's hair, more lines around his eyes and mouth than she remembered. A pang of guilt darted through her.

"I don't believe we've met," he said to Spence, "even though you do look familiar to me."

"This is Spencer Bishop, Dad. Anthony's brother."

Natalie felt more than saw her father's slight hesitation before he extended his hand to Spence. The two men shook hands, then her dad said, "Come on into the living room. Your mother's out in the kitchen. I'd better go get her or she'll have my hide."

Natalie said, "Where's Kyle?"

"He's out back feeding your mother's dog. I'll get him, too." Her mother's dog was a ten-year-old keeshond that had been a part of the Silver family since the day he was born. But her father never referred to him as anything but "your mother's dog," even though he was just as crazy about Major as the rest of them were.

Just then, the kitchen door swung open and Natalie's mother came through. "Paul, I thought I heard voices—" She saw Natalie and her eyes lit up with happiness. "Natalie!"

Mother and daughter met halfway across the room and flung their arms around each other. Natalie had to lean down to embrace her mother. Trim, petite, a bundle of energy, Joy Silver looked at least ten years younger than her fifty-two years. Her hair was darker than Natalie's, her eyes a different shade of blue, but there was still a strong resemblance between them.

"Oh, my God," her mother cried. "I didn't think we would be able to get you out until tomorrow. It broke my heart, thinking about you spending the night in that horrible place. But I should have known your father would come up with some way to get you out. Why didn't you tell me?" she asked, craning her head around Natalie to stare accusingly at her husband.

"Because I didn't know," her father said. "I'm not the one who posted her bail."

"Then who did?" her mother demanded.

"Actually... it was Spence who posted the bail."

"Spence?"

Natalie looped her arm through her mother's and pulled her forward. "This is Spencer Bishop, Mom. Anthony's brother."

Her mother's hand fluttered to her heart. "Oh, my," she murmured. Her gaze flew to her husband's, and Natalie saw her father's shoulders lift in a slight shrug as if to say, *I'm as confused by all this as you are.*

As if sensing the undercurrents, Spence said, "I should be shoving off. I'm sure the three of you must have a lot to talk about."

"You don't want to do that," her father said.

"I beg your pardon?"

"You don't want to leave before you have a chance to see your nephew."

Spence looked at Natalie, who quickly glanced away.

"Some other time, perhaps—" he started.

"We don't want to hold you up any longer—" Natalie began.

"Mom! You're back!"

Before either of them could say another word, Kyle, dressed in a San Antonio Spurs sweatshirt, blue jeans, and sneakers, sprang through the kitchen door and launched himself at Natalie. She caught him in her arms, twirling him around and around until both of them collapsed on the plaid sofa, dizzy and laughing.

"I missed you so much," she said, kissing his cheek, but he was already pushing her slightly away as he turned to stare at Spence.

Green eyes met green eyes.

They measured each other for a long moment before Kyle wiggled off Natalie's lap and sat on the couch beside her. "You look like my father," he said.

Natalie's gaze flew to Spence's. He was studying Kyle just as intently as Kyle was studying him. From where Natalie sat, their profiles looked identical. But then, all the Bishops looked alike.

"I'm your uncle," Spence said. "Your father's brother. It's nice to finally meet you."

"You're not here to take my mother away again, are you?" Kyle demanded, his eyes narrowing on Spence.

Spence looked slightly startled, then said, "No. I brought her home, so you could take care of her."

Kyle pondered this, then nodded, seemingly satisfied with the answer. "Good," he said. "That's good."

"Would you like something to drink, Spence?" her mother asked, having gotten over her initial shock. "Hot chocolate or wassail, perhaps?"

Spence turned to her. "No, thanks. I really do have to be going."

"Let me walk you out." Her father put his hand on Spence's shoulder. The two of them turned toward the front door, and Natalie could hear her father speaking in a low voice as they stood in the foyer before Spence departed. She couldn't help wondering what her father was saying to him. And what Spence was saying in return.

As if drawn by her intense scrutiny, Spence turned at the door. His gaze captured Natalie's and her breath caught in her throat. She asked herself again, what he was doing here? Why he had bailed her out?

Dear God, she thought, what was he up to?

SPENCE PAUSED ON THE porch, unsettled by his brief encounter with the Silvers. The night suddenly seemed cold and bleak compared to the warmth he'd just left behind. For a moment, he had the strongest urge to turn around and go back, to join them in their cozy little domain, but there was no place for him inside that house. No place for him anywhere.

He'd always told himself that, in his line of work, it was better not to have ties. Better not to have a family—people who depended on you coming home every night.

He told himself that same thing now, but he couldn't seem to shake the disquiet that being with Natalie's family had awakened in him.

Starting across the yard toward his car, he glanced back, unable to resist. Through the large front window, he could see clearly into the house. He felt like a voyeur, but he couldn't seem to tear his gaze away.

The Silvers had all grouped themselves around the fireplace. Paul was seated in an overstuffed chair, while his wife perched on the arm. Joy. What an apt name, he thought, seeing the woman's smile flash down at her husband.

Spence thought that looking at Joy Silver was probably like getting a glimpse of what Natalie would look like in twenty years. They had the same bone structure, were both very thin and petite, and they both had the same soul-melting smile.

Natalie was seated on the floor in front of her father's chair with Kyle on her lap, her arms wrapped tightly around him, as if she would never let him go. But she was gazing up at her father, obviously clinging to every word Paul spoke.

In the split second that Spence stood gazing inside that window, it seemed to him that Paul Silver must be the luckiest man in the world.

"NATALIE? YOU STILL UP?"

Natalie turned from the window in her parents' guest room as her father poked his head inside the door. "Come in, Daddy."

Paul, dressed in dark blue pajamas and robe, crossed the room to stand at the window beside her. They stood silently for a few minutes, gazing at the Christmas lights on the house across the street.

Finally her father said, "What do you know about this Spencer Bishop?"

"Not much," Natalie hedged.

"I can't help worrying about his motives. If he's anything like Anthony, I can't see him doing anything out of the goodness of his heart."

"I know," Natalie said. "That worries me, too."

"Then you don't trust him?"

She shrugged. "I can't afford to. I can't afford to trust anyone right now, except you and Mom and

Kyle." She turned to her father, gazing up at him earnestly. "I'm so sorry about...all this. All the trouble I've caused."

"Now, you listen to me," he said sternly. "This is not your fault. Any of it."

"I know, but if I'd never married Anthony—"

"You wouldn't have that great little guy in the next room. Think about that."

Natalie turned back to stare out the window. She'd thought of little else but Kyle since this whole ordeal had begun.

Paul put his arm around her and drew her close. "This family's been through a lot over the years, and we've always come through just fine. We'll get through this just like we've gotten through everything else—by sticking together. You hear me?"

Natalie smiled at the gruffness in his tone. "I hear you."

"Okay." He squeezed her arm. "Try to get a good night's sleep. Things always seem brighter in the morning."

At the door, he turned back suddenly.

"Natalie, about the bail..."

"What about it?"

He paused, then said, "You know I would have sold my soul to get you out of that place, don't you?"

Her eyes filled with tears. "I know that."

He nodded. "'Night."

"Good night, Daddy."

Chapter Five

Sunlight streamed in through the tall windows in the morning room, highlighting the silver streaks in Irene Bishop's perfectly coifed blond hair. She sat on the very edge of a tapestried armchair, her posture stick straight, her bearing regal, her air one of aloofness. She resembled her surroundings, Spence thought, not for the first time. Beautiful, elegant, and completely untouchable.

"Thank you for coming by so early this morning, Spencer," she said formally.

"How are you feeling?"

"How would you expect me to feel? My son has been brutally murdered." But whatever grief she might have been experiencing was carefully masked behind the perfect makeup, the perfect hairdo, the perfect black dress.

"I'm sorry," he said inadequately. "I know how difficult this must be for you."

"You have no idea," she replied, still without so much as a quiver of emotion in her voice or expression. Although he did notice that the hand holding the fragile ivory demitasse trembled as she lifted it to her lips. She took a delicate sip, then set the cup down on a marble-topped table. "The funeral is set for tomorrow. All the arrangements have been made. Only close friends and family and, of course, a few of Anthony's most trusted associates will be invited.''

Who, in their right mind, had trusted Anthony? Spence wondered, then immediately felt guilty. His brother had been dead for little more than twenty-four hours. Couldn't he find it in himself to show even an ounce of compassion, one measure of regret?

Spence turned away from his mother, his gaze going automatically to the portrait of his father and brother that hung over the marble fireplace. Anthony, Sr., was seated, while his favorite son stood slightly behind him, one hand resting on his father's shoulder. They stared down from their lofty position with the same handsome face, the same arrogant expression, the same cool green eyes.

The same eyes Spence saw when he looked at himself in the mirror.

But the similarities between him and Anthony—or with any of the other Bishops—ended there. Or at least Spence had always told himself so. He'd always told himself he was different, and that was the reason he was treated like an outsider in his own family. That was the reason there wasn't a single Bishop he'd ever been close to. Not his mother, not his sister, and especially not his brother.

He and Anthony had never gotten along, even as children. But seven years ago, when Spence had learned of Anthony's treachery and Natalie's betrayal, he'd known then that there would never be a reconciliation between his brother and him. Their differences were too great. The paths they'd each chosen for themselves, too divergent.

And now it was too late.

He rubbed his face with both hands as he turned back to Irene. "Is that why you wanted to see me this morning? To tell me about the arrangements?"

"You're her son," Anthea said from the doorway. "Does she need a reason other than that?"

She always has before, Spence thought bitterly, glancing up to find his sister glaring at him from the doorway.

She walked into the room, tall and thin, head held high, striving to attain the Bishop air, but somehow not quite managing to pull it off.

Perhaps it was the almost-imperceptible slump of her shoulders, Spence thought. Or perhaps the way her suit—no doubt expensive—hung on her lanky frame like a bag. Her dark hair was cut in a short, boyish style that did nothing to soften her angular features. But, even given all that, she might still have been mildly attractive if not for the permanent scowl that darkened her face.

Anthea Bishop possessed not one ounce of her mother's sense of style or elegance, and Irene never seemed to let her forget it. Her critical gaze measured her daughter's progress across the room, but she said nothing. She didn't have to. Her silent disapproval echoed like a scream.

Spence could almost feel sorry for his sister. He'd been on the receiving end of Irene's cold disapproval far more times than he cared to remember. Only when she had looked at Anthony had her eyes lit with an inner glow. Only then had Spence ever glimpsed an emotion that remotely resembled maternal pride.

But instead of their lowly positions in the family drawing them closer together, Spence and Anthea were hardly more than strangers to each other. While Spence had compensated for the lack of parental affection by becoming wild and rebellious in his teenage years, then later pulling away from the family altogether, Anthea had become cold and sullen, steadfastly clinging to her heritage as a Bishop. She was forty-one years old and still living at home with her mother.

His sister's cool, assessing eyes seemed to challenge him now, although Spence had no idea what she might be thinking. He'd never been able to read Anthea.

"The reason I wanted to see you this morning," Irene was saying, "is because I'd like for you to come home, Spencer."

He gazed down at her in surprise. "What do you mean, come home?"

"I'd like for you to move back into this house, with Anthea and me."

His surprise turned to astonishment, and he found himself at a complete loss for words. He wondered fleetingly what his mother would think if she knew the real reason he'd come back to San Antonio; if she found out that his assignment had been to get Jack Russo at any cost, even if it meant implicating his own brother in a crime so dark and vile, the Bishop name would never again be the same.

Spence didn't think she would be inviting him to move back home, that was for sure.

"I told you yesterday I'm only here for the holidays. I live in Washington."

"I'm aware of that." Rising, Irene walked to the window and parted the heavy brocade curtains to gaze out at the sunlit courtyard.

She's still so beautiful, Spence thought, watching her. He'd once thought her the most beautiful woman in the world. Her figure was still straight and slender, her hair still thick and lush. The only thing that gave away her age was the blue-veined hand that trembled on the curtain.

He remembered how unblemished and elegant her hands had once been. How, as a child, he had admired the way her diamond rings sparkled against their ivory smoothness. How he had longed to have those hands smooth back his hair, soothe away his tears . . .

Irene let the curtain fall back into place and turned to him. "It may surprise you to learn that I've kept abreast of your career, Spencer. I know you've done quite well for yourself with the FBI. I'm told you're a very good agent."

Spence lifted an eyebrow at her placating tone, automatically suspicious of his mother's motives. Across the room, Anthea watched him carefully, her expression grim.

"Of course, it certainly isn't the profession your father or I would have chosen for you," Irene continued. "But you always were headstrong. You always did have your own way of doing things. You never wanted to listen to your father or to me about anything."

Maybe because you never listened to me. But that was old ground and Spence had no intention of covering it again. "I made the decision that was right for me," he said. "I was never cut out to be a lawyer."

A spark of something that might have been anger flashed in Irene's light blue eyes. As if to hide the betraying emotion, she turned back to the window. "Ironically, it's because of your job, Spencer, because of who you are and what you do, that makes me ask this of you now. I want you to move back into this house until after the trial. I want you to promise me that you will do everything you can to bring Natalie Silver to justice."

Spence stared at his mother's back, telling himself he was a fool to feel disappointed. What had he thought? That she'd wanted him to move back home so she could take some measure of comfort or solace from his presence? That in losing one son, she'd realized she still had another?

He should have known better.

"I don't trust the local authorities," she said. "Neither your father nor your brother had the slightest bit of confidence in the police department. There has always been too much corruption, too many officers willing to take a bribe—or have their heads turned by a pretty face. I won't allow that to happen in this case."

It was pointless to argue with her, so all Spence said was, "And where do I come in?"

She faced him. "You have experience dealing with this sort of thing. In your line of work, you've conducted investigations not unlike the one involving Anthony's murder."

He waited, saying nothing. He could feel Anthea's eyes, boring into his back, and he wondered what she thought. Had she known Irene's intentions? Or was all this as much a surprise to her as it was to Spence?

He glanced at her, but her expression gave away nothing.

Suddenly Irene's composure snapped. She took a step toward him, her eyes blazing with rage. "I want you to follow this investigation yourself, Spencer. I want you to use your contacts in the police department to find out everything you can about this case. I want you to make sure *that woman* doesn't get off on some kind of trumped-up technicality."

Irene lifted her wrinkled hand, as if to touch him, and the emerald-cut diamond on her finger emitted a cold, white light. Once he would have been mesmerized by the movement of her hand reaching out to him, but now Spence saw no beauty in the gesture at all, just a grotesque reminder of what might have been.

As if realizing the same thing, Irene let her hand fall back to her side.

"I want that woman put away for life," she said. "I want her confined to a cold, dark cell with no hope of salvation. I want her to spend every waking hour remembering what she did to my son. What she did to this family. I want her to suffer, Spencer. I want to take her son from her just like she took mine."

Spence glared down at her. "What are you saying?"

"The boy. Kyle. I want to take him away from her. I want that woman to know what it's like to lose her only son."

"Anthony wasn't your only son, Mother," Spence replied, his voice taut with anger.

"Of course not," Irene said, having the grace at least to look slightly ruffled at her slip, but she almost immediately regained her composure. "You are my son, too, Spencer. My only son now, and I'm counting on you to help me. Natalie Silver will rot in prison for the rest of her life. And, just like me, she will never see her son again."

"WHAT A DILEMMA this must be for you."

Spence turned from the window where he'd been standing since his mother had left a few minutes ago to go upstairs and rest. Anthea had gone, too, but now she was back, and by the sound of the sarcasm in her voice, she was spoiling for a fight.

"What do you mean?"

She smiled smugly, reminding him of Anthony. "I mean, considering how you felt about 'that woman.' I remember when you first met her. I saw the way you looked at her that day, the way you couldn't take your eyes off her. Still can't, for all we know."

Spence remembered the day he'd met Natalie, too. She'd been nineteen, a student working her way through Trinity University with a part-time job at his family's law firm. And Spence had been twenty-three, fresh out of Quantico, a rookie agent out to make a name for himself on his first big case.

He was on assignment in San Antonio, and word had reached his father that he was in town. Anthony, Sr., had summoned Spence to his law office, and he'd reluctantly gone.

Natalie had been working with his father's assistant in the outer office, and from the moment Spence had laid eyes on her, he'd known there was something very special about Natalie Silver, something so appealing about the way her soft, brown hair framed her lovely face and the way her blue eyes shimmered behind the wire-rimmed glasses she wore. And her smile. That shy, sweet smile that stole his breath away.

The chemistry between them had been immediate and explosive, leading to the inevitable. But their brief affair might have become, after all these years, nothing more than a bittersweet memory...if Natalie hadn't gone and done the unforgivable.

If she hadn't betrayed him with his own brother.

His voice took on a bitter edge when he said, "You've got this all wrong, Anthea. Natalie Silver means nothing to me. She never did."

"Oh, really? Then why did you bail her out of jail? Oh, yes, I know all about that." Anthea gloated, her green eyes gleaming with satisfaction. "You're not the only one with connections at the police department, you know."

"Why didn't you tell Mother?" Spence demanded, studying his sister carefully. Something had changed about Anthea, but he couldn't quite put his finger on it.

"Oh, I plan to," she said. "When it suits me. *If* it suits me." She smiled again, and suddenly Spence knew what it was that was different about his sister. Her defiance. Her confidence. Her whole demeanor. Anthea was no longer the meek, mild sister who had lived all her life in her brother's shadow. She was no longer a pale, faded copy of her twin but was now the only original.

And she liked it, Spence realized. She liked it very much.

"Just think about it," Anthea told him. "For the first time in your life, you have a chance to win our dear mother's undying gratitude and admiration. And all you have to do is put away for life a woman you were once in love with. All you have to do is take away Natalie Silver's son."

She laughed, lifting her hands to study them intently. "Now, granted, that would have been a piece of cake for Anthony, but what about you, Spencer? Can you keep an open mind about this case? Or will you let your feelings for 'that woman' undermine your loyalty to your family?"

Her voice had turned into a taunt, grating on Spence's nerves. He gave her a cool, cynical appraisal that did justice to his last name. "You don't have to worry about me, Anthea. No one could ever make me change the way I feel about my family."

THE DAY OF ANTHONY'S funeral dawned warm and sunny with the high expected to be around eighty. It didn't seem at all like Christmas to Natalie, but she knew her flagging spirits had very little to do with the soaring temperature, and everything to do with the fact that she'd been charged with her ex-husband's murder.

She was truly sorry Anthony was dead. At times, she'd hated him during their short marriage. She'd despised his coldness and the cruel streak he kept so cleverly hidden. Later, she'd detested his careless disregard for her son's feelings. But no matter what Anthony had done, no matter how bitterly they had disagreed on just about everything, she had never wanted him dead.

The house seemed so silent this morning, Natalie thought, wrapping her arms around herself as she stared out the window. She saw her neighbor pass by, walking her dog, and gaze toward Natalie's house. But instead of waving when she saw Natalie at the window, the woman turned and hurried down the street.

She thinks I did it, Natalie thought numbly. *She's known me for almost five years, and now, suddenly, she thinks I'm a cold-blooded killer.*

Her neighbor wasn't the only one who thought so. Yesterday, when Natalie and Kyle had moved back to their own house, the phone had rung nonstop. Some of the callers were well-wishers—friends and family who still had faith in her—but most of the calls had been from reporters wanting a sensational story, or from crackpots who wanted the perverse thrill of talking to someone they thought was a murderer.

Natalie shuddered. She'd called the phone company to get an unlisted number to try and halt the barrage. Only her parents and her attorney knew her new number, and so far, the morning had been blessedly quiet.

Almost too quiet. She wished she could go back to work, but her shop was still considered a crime scene. No one except authorized police personnel were allowed in or out, while Silver Bells's Christmas sales slowly went down the drain.

The period between Thanksgiving and Christmas comprised a good thirty-five percent of Natalie's annual sales. The last week of November and the first two weeks of December had been so promising this year, and she'd hoped to show her biggest profit ever.

But even when she was allowed to reopen the store, what then? Would the customers come back? Or had the publicity surrounding Anthony's murder and her arrest driven them all away?

Don't think about that now, Natalie advised herself sternly as she heard Kyle walk into the room. There was nothing she could do about it, so why waste time worrying? Especially when she had so many other things to worry about.

She forced herself to smile as Kyle came to stand in front of her for inspection. She bent to adjust his tie.

"It's choking me," he complained, pulling on the tie the moment Natalie finished straightening it.

"Leave it alone, Kyle," she said in exasperation. "Pulling on it just makes it tighter." She gave it another adjustment, then stood back and studied him. "You look very handsome."

Kyle screwed up his freshly scrubbed face. The freckles on his nose stood out like tiny copper coins. "I look like a dork."

"No, you don't. And quit messing with your hair. It took me ten minutes to get all the cowlicks to lie down."

"Well, what *can* I do?" he asked in frustration. "I can't ride my bike. I can't go skating. I can't even go to school."

"You can sit there and wait for your grandmother's car to come pick you up," Natalie said, trying to keep the heaviness out of her voice.

When Irene Bishop had called yesterday, before Natalie's number was changed, to say that she wanted Kyle to accompany the family to the funeral today, Natalie's first instinct had been to refuse. But then, she knew that wouldn't be right. Later, Kyle might have wondered why she had kept him from Anthony's funeral. He might have one day regretted it, and Natalie didn't want that. Letting Kyle go to the funeral was the decent thing to do, and so she'd finally agreed.

Irene told her that Anthea would accompany their driver to pick Kyle up this morning, and they would deliver him home again after the service. Then she had hung up without another word.

As if sensing his mother's dread, Kyle said, "I don't want to go."

"I know, but we talked about this last night, remember? It's the right thing to do." Natalie took his hand and held it between hers. "Your grandmother needs you. Your being there today will help her a lot."

"Why can't you go with me?"

"Because . . . that wouldn't be the right thing to do."

"Because you and my dad were divorced?"

"That's . . . part of it."

"Because you don't like Grandmother Bishop?"

Natalie looked at him in shock. "I never said that."

He shrugged. "It's okay. I don't like her, neither."

"Kyle!"

"Well, I don't," he said defiantly. "And she can't make me like her."

"Oh, Kyle." Natalie didn't know what to say to her son; how to explain to him the difficulties she had with the Bishops. She'd told him very little of the ordeal she'd been through since Anthony's death, only that the police had wanted to ask her some questions because they were trying to figure out exactly what had happened to Anthony.

But children were a lot smarter and more perceptive than adults gave them credit for, and Kyle was no exception. Natalie had a feeling he knew a good deal more about what was going on than he was letting on, and she thought that he was probably a lot more upset than he seemed. But he was a Bishop. He didn't like to show emotion.

"Kyle—" She wasn't sure what she'd been about to say to him, but just then she heard a car outside. She got up and went to the window. A black limo pulled up to the curb and the driver got out to open the back door.

Natalie turned back to Kyle. "Your aunt's here to pick you up." She knelt to straighten his tie once again. "Now, I want you to be a good boy, okay?"

He nodded. Suddenly, his green eyes looked suspiciously bright. "Why can't you come with me?" he asked again.

"It'll be okay," she promised. "I'll be here waiting for you when you get back."

She stood then and went to answer the doorbell. When she drew back the door, her hand flew to her heart in surprise. "Oh! It's...you. I was expecting Anthea."

"Something came up," Spence said. "Anthea couldn't make it."

Natalie wondered uneasily if something had really come up, or if Spence had engineered this whole thing himself, just to be with Kyle. But then, why would he? He didn't even know her son.

She chided herself for her suspicions, but like it or not, she didn't trust Spencer Bishop. He'd bailed her out of jail, and Natalie still couldn't help wondering why.

Reluctantly, she let her gaze travel over him. He was dressed in a dark suit, a white shirt, and a somber silk tie. Like Kyle, his dark hair looked freshly dampened and combed, as tamed as it probably ever would be. He wore it a little shorter than she remembered, but it was still thick, without a trace of gray, and she wondered suddenly if he remembered the way she had once run her fingers through those dark, unruly strands. If he remembered the way—

She stopped, gazing up at him. Her pulse hammered in her throat, for she suddenly remembered something else about Spence—that he had always been able to read her thoughts.

"No one told me about this change of plans," she said coldly.

"Is there a problem?" Spence asked. "What difference does it make who takes him to the church?"

"It makes a difference to me. I should have been told."

"Why? Don't you trust me with your son?"

Before she could answer, Natalie felt Kyle lean against her leg, and she reached down automatically to put her arm around his shoulders—to draw him close, to protect him.

"Hi," he said.

"Hi," Spence said.

"Do I get to ride in that big car out there?"

"You sure do. That is, if your mother says it's okay." Spence's gaze challenged hers.

"Does it have a TV?" Kyle asked.

"Yeah, it does."

"Wow," Kyle said, taking a step or two away from Natalie to stare out the door at the big black limo waiting at the curb.

Resentment flooded through her. It was so easy to turn a young boy's head with a fancy car. She wondered if Spence had deliberately tried to do just that.

She lifted her chin and met Spence's gaze. "I want him home as soon as the service is over."

Something flashed in Spence's eyes. Something that made Natalie want to snatch her son back inside, and never let him go. Then Spence said, "You don't have to worry about Kyle. I'll take good care of him."

Leaning down, she gave her son a quick hug. "I'll see you in a little while," she whispered.

"Okay." He hugged her back, then, without another word, followed Spence outside.

Natalie stood at the door and watched the two of them walk away. Spence and her son.

It'll only be for an hour or two, she told herself. What could happen in such a short time? Kyle would go to Anthony's funeral, and then her son would come back home to her and the two of them would get on with their lives and never have to deal with the Bishops again.

But as she watched Spence and Kyle disappear inside the car, Natalie was suddenly overcome by a premonition, a dark feeling that her son was in danger... and there was nothing she could do about it.

THE MOMENT THEY JOINED the rest of the family at the church, Spence sensed Kyle's panic. Everyone kept staring at him, shaking their heads and whispering behind gloved hands. No wonder the little guy looked a little green around the gills, Spence thought. The Bishops and their entourage were a bit much for anyone to take.

He bent down and said in Kyle's ear, "Let's get some air."

Kyle nodded, obviously relieved. He followed Spence outside into a walled courtyard. Spence sat down on a stone bench near a fountain and Kyle did the same. For several moments they said nothing, just sat there staring into the water.

Finally, Spence said, "It's all right if you're feeling a little scared about all this."

Kyle turned his green eyes on him but said nothing.

"It's even okay," Spence added quietly, "if you feel like crying. It's perfectly natural in this situation."

"But I don't," Kyle replied. His gaze dropped to his shoes. He studied them intently. "That's the problem," he muttered.

"What is?"

"I don't feel like crying. I don't feel sad or anything."

So that was it. Spence thought it was probably appropriate that Kyle was talking to him about all this. If anyone in the world could understand the boy's confusion, his conflicting emotions about his father, it was Spence. Anthony's brother.

"I think I see what you mean," he said. "You didn't know your father very well, did you?"

Kyle shook his head, his eyes still on his shoes.

"That wasn't your fault, you know. It was his. He chose not to be a part of your life for a very long time. There's no reason for you to feel guilty. About anything. Do you understand what I'm saying?"

"I think so." Kyle fell silent for a moment, then turned suddenly to Spence, squinting in the dappled sunlight. "Do *you* feel sad?"

"In some ways," he said honestly. Anthony hadn't been an easy man to know or to love, but he'd still been Spence's brother and, like it or not, there had still been a bond between them.

A bond that Spence had been perfectly willing to break, all in the name of justice.

"My mom's sad," Kyle was saying. "I heard her crying last night when she thought I was asleep."

Spence didn't like to picture Natalie crying. He didn't like to think about her alone and frightened, vulnerable.

Better to remember the woman who had betrayed him. The woman who had chosen his brother over him.

"Mom doesn't like for me to see her cry," Kyle said solemnly. "She doesn't want me to worry about her."

"Well, that's the way mothers are," Spence said. He grinned, trying to lighten the moment. "It's kind of a 'mother thing,' you know?"

Kyle grinned back, displaying the gap created by his two missing front teeth. "Yeah," he said. "It's kind of a 'mother thing.'" He started to say something else, then his eyes widened and he pointed over Spence's shoulder. "Hey! There's a guy hiding in the bushes over there! Look!"

Spence whirled in time to see a man spring out of a clump of oleander and sprint toward the stone wall, a camera and an equipment bag slung over his shoulder.

Without thinking, Spence took off after him. He caught the man before he could make his getaway.

Spence whirled the man around, grabbing a fistful of his shirt. "What the hell are you doing here?"

"Just taking a few pictures," he gasped. "I work for the *Scimitar*. I didn't mean any harm—just trying to get a story. That kid over there's Anthony Bishop's son, isn't he?"

"That kid over there is my nephew, and I don't like scum like you sneaking around taking his picture." Spence's blood boiled at the thought of a stranger, a reporter bent only on getting a story, eavesdropping on his and Kyle's private conversation. A conversation that had meant a lot to him, although he couldn't say why, exactly.

"Is it true the kid's mother whacked Bishop?"

The guy never even saw it coming. Spence's fist shot out and connected with the reporter's face. He fell sprawling to the ground. "My nose! You broke my nose, you son of a bitch!"

Spence reached down and grabbed the camera.

"Hey! What do you think you're doing?"

Calmly, Spence opened the back of the camera and removed the film, exposing it to light.

Outraged, the reporter leaped to his feet. "You can't do that!" he screamed, holding his nose.

"I just did. Now you get the hell out of here and don't ever let me catch you hanging around my nephew again."

"I'll sue you for every penny you've got. Not even a Bishop can get away with this. You haven't heard the last of me!" The man spouted a string of obscenities as he took his camera and ruined film and climbed over the wall with as much dignity as he could muster. Which wasn't much, in Spence's opinion.

He walked back over to Kyle, who sat gazing up at him in awe. "Did that guy really take a picture of me? Is that really why you hit him?"

Spence grinned and shrugged. "Yeah. I guess you could say it was kind of an 'uncle thing' to do."

"Awesome," Kyle said. "I sure hope I get to be an uncle someday."

KYLE HAD BEEN GONE little more than an hour when the phone rang. Thinking it was probably her mother or possibly her attorney, Natalie picked up without hesitation.

"Hello?"

There was a pause, then a male voice said gruffly, "You've got something of mine, lady."

"I beg your pardon?"

"You know what I'm talking about. You've got something of mine, and I want them back."

A finger of dread crawled up Natalie's spine. "How did you get this number?"

"Let's just say, I've got friends in high places."

"Who are you?"

"You don't need to know who I am. It's enough that I know who you are. I know all about you, Natalie, because I've been watching you. I know where you live, I know where you work, and I know where your kid is at this very moment."

Natalie gasped. "Who are you?" she cried. "What do you want?"

"You know what I want. I want what's mine. Cooperate, and nobody else has to get hurt."

The phone clicked, then went dead in her ear.

Natalie sat holding the receiver for a long moment, her hand shaking in fear. She wanted to believe it was just another crank call, but she didn't dare. Not when her son had just been threatened.

Natalie started to panic. How could she have let Kyle out of her sight for even a minute? What had she been thinking? What if someone came up to him at the funeral, threatened him somehow? There would be no one around to protect him. Certainly not Irene or Anthea—two colder women Natalie had never had the misfortune of knowing. And Spence? He was a Bishop, wasn't he? She couldn't exactly rely on him.

She thought about calling the police, but what if they didn't believe her? What if they thought she'd made the whole thing up, just to try and throw suspicion off herself? They didn't even believe Anthony had ransacked her workroom that night. Sergeant Phillips had suggested she'd done it herself, just to throw them off track.

No, she couldn't call the police. She wasn't even sure there was cause for alarm, but before she had time to talk herself out of what she was contemplating, Natalie grabbed her purse and car keys and headed for the garage. Within minutes she was driving out of her neighborhood, fighting the heavy Christmas-shopping traffic on the freeway.

She glanced at her watch. The church service would be over, and the mourners would be on their way to the cemetery by now. But as she pulled into the parking area at Oak Lawn Cemetery, where the Bishops had an enormous mausoleum, she saw that the funeral procession had already arrived.

Natalie got out of her car and walked toward the gates. She had no intention of interrupting the service.

She only wanted to see Kyle from a distance, make sure he was okay. She could remain where she was and watch over him, and no one would ever have to know.

But as she stood there in the cool shade of a water oak, a chill crept over her. She turned and saw that she was the one who was being watched.

For a moment, he looked so much like Anthony that Natalie's breath rushed out of her in a painful gasp. Then she realized it was Spence, and her heartbeat slowed. But only temporarily. The moment he started toward her, her blood began to pound again.

He looked so menacing, she thought. So...dangerous. His green eyes flashed with anger, and his heavy eyebrows were drawn together in a scowl. Although it was early, she could see the faint trace of beard that shadowed his face, making him seem even darker. More threatening. Never had his presence affected her more powerfully than it did at that moment. Natalie stared up at him, as if mesmerized.

But when he spoke, his voice, as threatening as his thunderous appearance, broke the spell. "What the hell are you doing here?"

"I...came to see Kyle," she said. "I wanted to make sure he was all right."

"Why wouldn't he be all right?"

"Reporters have been hounding us since I got out of jail. We've been getting a lot of prank calls. I didn't want him to get upset if...someone said something to him. About what happened."

Spence glared at her. "I don't have to tell you how upset my family would be if they saw you here. This wasn't a good idea, Natalie."

"Maybe not," she retorted. "But I've done a lot of things in my life that weren't such hot ideas. That's never stopped me before."

He lifted his eyebrows in a challenge. "Like killing my brother?"

Her face colored with anger. "Like *marrying* him," she countered. "Like getting involved with *you.*" The moment the words were out, she regretted them. Regretted the power they gave him over her. Because now he knew she hadn't forgotten him or the brief relationship they'd once shared. Now he knew that he had once hurt her deeply, and that she had never gotten over it.

"*Involved?*" He laughed. "Your memories are kinder than mine. I thought we had an affair. A one-night stand."

Before she thought, Natalie's hand lifted to slap him, but he caught her wrist in mid-swing and stood staring down at her, his green eyes blazing with anger. "Do you think our *involvement* meant anything to me? Do you think I've wasted one minute thinking about you? Thinking about the way you married my brother the minute my back was turned? You and Anthony deserved each other. You were perfect for each other. You both knew exactly what you wanted and how to get it, and you didn't care who you stepped on in the process."

His words would have been like nails hammered into her heart, except for one thing—except for the glimmer of hurt in the depths of his eyes, belying his bitter words.

Natalie saw that hurt and recognized it for what it was, because she'd seen it in her own eyes. More times than she cared to remember.

"You're the one who left," she whispered.

"Not that it matters," he said, "but I left because I had an assignment. I was called back to Washington. I told you that. I told you I wouldn't be able to see you for a while—"

"Because you were working *under cover?*"

He frowned at her sarcastic emphasis. "Yes."

She laughed bitterly. "It may surprise you to learn that I knew all about that little undercover assignment of yours. I even saw pictures."

He gazed down at her in astonishment. "What the hell are you talking about?"

"Anthony told me all about it. He said—"

Although Spence had been gazing at her intently, his attention suddenly shifted to somewhere over her right shoulder. A commotion sounded behind her—fierce whispers, the rustle of silk—and Natalie whirled, coming face-to-face with the three Bishop women leaving the cemetery.

They were all dressed in black, all wore veils, and as she gazed at them, a line from *Macbeth* flashed through Natalie's mind: "By the pricking of my thumbs,/ Something wicked this way comes."

Enter three witches.

Irene, the undisputed leader of the coven, stopped dead in her tracks when she saw Natalie. She lifted her veil to rake her former daughter-in-law with icy contempt. The black dress she wore was stark, except for the pearl choker, trimmed with diamonds, that glittered at her throat.

Beside Irene, clad in a short black dress that displayed a shocking amount of black-stockinged leg, Melinda Bishop, the grieving widow, clutched Irene's arm with one gloved hand. Her red curls were piled under a wide-brimmed black hat, and dark glasses shielded her eyes. Natalie couldn't tell if Melinda was looking at her or not.

On the other side of Irene stood Anthea, also dressed in black, but her face and her bearing held none of her mother's regal elegance. Instead, Anthea looked like a pale copy of Anthony.

Once Natalie had gotten to know the Bishops, she'd learned quickly that Anthony was the only offspring who meant anything to Irene. She'd adored her eldest son while merely tolerating Anthea who, in spite of her brilliance, was obviously a huge disappointment.

Spence, Anthony had once told Natalie, had been disowned by the time he was eighteen because of his failure to conform to Bishop standards.

And yet, here he was today, the very picture of solidarity as he walked over to his mother. For some reason she couldn't fathom, Natalie felt oddly betrayed.

When Kyle saw Natalie, he rushed toward her. "Mommy!"

Natalie met him, bending to wrap her arms around him. He clung to her for a moment, then gazed up at her. "Can we go home now? Please?"

She smoothed back his hair. "Yes."

Melinda took off her dark glasses, her gaze scouring Natalie with scorn. "How dare you come here like this? Have you no shame?"

Natalie stood, clutching Kyle's hand. "I might ask you the same thing." She met Melinda's gaze evenly, until the grieving widow had to look away. Natalie thought she detected a hint of a blush on Melinda's face beneath the veil, but that was probably assuming too much. That was assuming Melinda Bishop had a conscience, and obviously she never had. How else could she have let her best friend pour out her heart and soul, while all the time having an affair with that same best friend's husband?

In some ways, Melinda's betrayal had hurt worse than Anthony's, because Natalie hadn't seen it coming. Right up to the bitter end, Melinda had pretended to care about Natalie, until she'd finally gotten what she wanted.

Natalie turned to Irene. "I'm sorry. I didn't mean to intrude. I only wanted to make sure my son was okay."

Kyle tugged frantically on Natalie's hand. "I want to go home, Mommy."

"We are, sweetheart." She turned to leave.

"One moment," Irene said.

Although the words were spoken softly, something in her tone stopped Natalie. She glanced back. Melinda was climbing into the back of the waiting limo, but Anthea remained at her mother's side, still as a statue. Her eyes—those Bishop eyes—bored into Natalie with open hostility.

For a moment, they all seemed frozen in time. Then Irene said, "I have something to say to you."

Spence was still standing beside Irene, but now he stepped forward, placing himself between her and Natalie. "This is not the time or place," he said harshly.

Irene spared him a brief glance. "It is exactly the time and place."

"Don't do this," Spence warned.

His voice sent shivers of alarm up Natalie's spine. Kyle pulled harder on her arm, as if he, too, sensed something was about to happen. "Mommy!"

Natalie put her arm around him, drawing him close. "It's okay, Kyle. Go wait for me in the car."

"But—"

"I'll be there in one minute. I promise."

Reluctantly, he did as he was told. Natalie could see her car from where she stood, and she watched as Kyle opened the door and climbed inside. Then she turned back to Irene.

"You were wise to wait and hear me out," Irene said. "I wouldn't have been pleased to have had to track you down to say what I have to say to you."

"Then say it," Natalie returned, bracing herself for another assault.

"Have you any idea what I'm feeling at this moment?" Irene asked, her cold blue eyes fixed on Natalie.

"I can only imagine," Natalie replied. "But I am truly sorry for your loss."

"Are you?"

"I didn't kill Anthony, Mrs. Bishop."

"Your innocence—or guilt—will be decided in a court of law. But even if a jury were to convict you, even if you were to spend the rest of your life behind bars, you still wouldn't know what I'm feeling. The kind of pain I've had to endure. The torment I've been put through. There's only one way that could happen."

Natalie's throat closed in fear. "What do you mean?"

Irene smiled slightly. "If you were to lose your child, your son, you would know then what I'm feeling at this moment."

Dear God, what was she saying? What was she threatening? Natalie's heart raced wildly. "You wouldn't hurt Kyle. He's just a baby—"

"You're right," Irene agreed, but there was something in her voice that chilled Natalie's blood. "I wouldn't hurt Kyle. He's my only grandson, my only link to Anthony. I wouldn't harm a single hair on his head, nor would I allow anyone else to.''

Natalie wanted to feel relief, but the icy blue eyes had narrowed to menacing slits. The blue-veined hands at Irene's sides balled into fists as her aristocratic face flashed with fury.

"I won't harm your son," she said softly. "But I will take him away from you. Only then will you know the pain and torment I've been put through. Only then will you have some inkling of the hell I'm going through now—and all because of you.''

Chapter Six

"Natalie!"

"Stay away from me!" she warned as she hurried across the parking lot to her car.

Spence caught up with her. "Wait a minute."

She spun to face him. "What for? So you can attack me again? So you and your mother can team up against me? You two make quite a pair."

"Look," he said, running his fingers through his dark hair. "Can we go somewhere and talk about this?"

"Why?"

"Because I can see you're upset."

"*Upset?*" She gazed at him in astonishment. "You think that's all I am? Your mother just threatened to take my son away from me. I'm a little more than upset."

He glanced away.

"You knew about this, didn't you?" Natalie demanded. "You knew what she was planning to do."

Spence rubbed the side of his face with his hand. He suddenly looked indescribably weary. "She mentioned it to me earlier."

"In front of Kyle?"

"No. The night after Anthony died."

A red veil of anger descended over Natalie as she glared up at him. "If you knew when you came to get Kyle what your mother was planning, why didn't you tell me? Didn't you think I had a right to know?"

"Yes. But I also didn't think you'd let him come if you knew."

"You were right about that," she answered coldly. "It's amazing how all you Bishops stick together. Blood certainly does tell, doesn't it?"

"I know how this must make you feel," Spence said carefully. "But try to look at this from her perspective. Her son is dead, and she thinks you killed him. Can you blame her for not wanting the woman she thinks is a murderess to raise her only grandson?"

"Don't you dare!" Natalie lashed out. "Don't you dare defend your mother to me. She doesn't care about Kyle. She only wants revenge against me. Well, let me tell you something. She will never get her hands on my son. She will never turn him into the kind of man Anthony was." *The kind of man you are,* she thought. "I'll do whatever it takes to stop her."

Spence's gaze hardened on her. "Is that how you felt when you found out Anthony was planning to sue you for custody of Kyle? Were you willing to do whatever it took to stop him?"

Natalie felt as if he had just punched her, very hard, in the stomach. Her breath left her in a painful rush. "I didn't kill Anthony," she said. "And I'm getting tired of having to tell you that. Why don't you just get out of my way and leave me alone?"

She tried to brush past him, but he caught her arm. "I can't do that."

"Why not? You obviously think I'm a murderer. Why waste your time with the likes of me?"

His green gaze darkened. "Because I told you before. I want answers, and you're the only one who can help me find them."

"Answers to *what?*" she cried in frustration. "I don't know anything. I was knocked unconscious while Anthony was being murdered. I didn't see or hear anything. I don't know anything, so just leave me and my son alone!"

She jerked her arm free of him and walked to the car door. Before she could open it, Spence said, "I'm not the one trying to take Kyle away from you, Natalie. I'm not your enemy."

Her gaze challenged his. "You're a Bishop, aren't you?"

"Yes," he said quietly. "But so is your son."

"DID SHE MEAN IT, MOM? Can she really take me away from you?"

Natalie looked down at Kyle in alarm. "Oh, honey, you heard all that?"

He shrugged sheepishly, but his eyes still looked frightened. "I rolled down my window."

"Kyle—"

"I know. I'm not supposed to eavesdrop. Are you mad at me?"

She smiled. "No, I'm not mad at you. I'm just sorry you had to hear all that. Your Grandmother Bishop is . . . very upset right now. She said a lot of things she didn't really mean." Or at least, Natalie prayed Irene hadn't meant them.

"She thinks you killed my dad, doesn't she?" The solemn little eyes, so innocent and trusting, gazed up at her.

Natalie bit back her tears and nodded.

The tips of Kyle's ears turned bright pink with anger. "I'd like to go punch her right in the nose."

Natalie put her fingertips to her lips, smiling. "That's the nicest thing anyone's said to me in a long time. Thank you, Kyle."

"You're welcome," he said earnestly. "I'd like to punch Anthea, too. But not Spence. I like him."

"You...do?"

"Yeah. He's way cool. He's not like the others. He talks to you and stuff. He doesn't just look at you. And he has a really neat car."

"The limo?"

"Naw, his real car. It's black and shiny and looks like a race car or something. It's fast as anything. He let me ride to the church with him in it, so I wouldn't have to go with the others. I hate the way they all stare at me, Mom. Especially *her.*"

"Which her?" Natalie started the car and drove out of the parking area.

"Melinda. I don't like her. And you know what?"

"What?"

"She doesn't like me."

Natalie glanced at her son. "I'm sure that's not true. She's upset now, too—"

He shook his head emphatically. "She didn't like me even before. I heard her say so to my dad once, when he took me to their house."

"You were in Melinda's house?"

Kyle nodded. "He told me not to tell you. He said it would be our secret."

That sounded like Anthony. Natalie's grip tightened on the steering wheel. "Did you and he have other secrets?"

Kyle turned to look out the side window. He said nothing.

"Well, did you?" Natalie persisted, feeling alarmed by her son's silence.

"Do you want to know what I heard her tell my dad or not?"

Natalie sighed. Like his father, Kyle had a neat way of changing the subject when it suited him. "What did she say?"

Kyle screwed up his face in concentration. "She said, 'How dare you bring that little brat into my home, flaunting him in my face when you know I can never have a baby of my own?'"

Natalie looked at him in shock. He'd mimicked Melinda's whining tone perfectly. "How do... How do you remember that conversation so well, honey?"

"I recorded it," he said proudly. "And I listened to it over and over. I thought it was funny."

"You recorded it? On that tape recorder your dad gave you?"

He nodded.

"I thought you said you lost it," Natalie reminded him. "You told me you couldn't find it anywhere."

Kyle looked stricken for a moment, as if realizing he'd given himself away, then said, "Well, that was before I lost it."

Natalie let that one pass for the moment. She braked for a light, automatically glancing in her rearview mirror. A black sports car pulled up behind her, but behind the tinted windshield, Natalie couldn't make out the driver.

"What did your dad say to Melinda?" she asked Kyle.

"He said he wanted a divorce."

"He did?"

"He told Melinda he wanted a divorce and he wasn't giving her any money. Or something like that."

"Kyle, are you sure about this?"

"I told you. I listened to it over and over. Melinda's got a really dumb voice, doesn't she, Mom?"

Natalie nodded absently. So Anthony had been ready to divorce Melinda, and she'd known it. Natalie wondered if the police had dug up that tidbit when they'd unearthed the fact that Anthony was going after custody of Kyle. Wouldn't that make Melinda an equal suspect?

Except, of course, for the fact that Melinda hadn't been found at the crime scene, holding the bloody murder weapon.

It all came back to that. Natalie had the feeling that the answer to all her troubles was hidden somewhere in the back of her mind, only there was no way she could get to it. No way she could find it. Because while Anthony was being murdered, she'd been out cold—

"Mom, look out!"

The light had turned green and she'd automatically entered the intersection. When she glanced over at Kyle's yell, she saw a car heading straight toward them.

It was too late to brake. The car would plow right into them on Kyle's side. Natalie did the only other thing she could do. She stepped on the gas and the car shot forward. But not before the other car had rammed the right rear fender of Natalie's car.

There was a terrible crunching sound, an awful bone-jarring impact and for a second, the steering wheel in Natalie's hand spun out of control. As if in a daze, she heard the distant sound of horns honking and tires squealing. Finally she managed to get the car stopped, and she sat for a moment, her head spinning.

Then she looked at Kyle. Even though he was wearing his seat belt, his head must have hit the side window on impact, because the window was shattered, and a stream of blood coursed down his face.

"Kyle! Oh, dear God." She fumbled with her seat belt, trying to free herself so she could reach for him.

"I'm hurt, Mommy!"

"I know, baby. Let me see how badly. Kyle, move your hand out of the way."

He brought his hand down from his face and gazed at it. "I'm bleeding!" he wailed. "I'm gonna die!"

Traffic was stopped all around them. They had been knocked out of the intersection, but the rear of the car still blocked one lane. "You're not going to die," Natalie told him, although her own heart was beating so hard she thought she might have a heart attack. "I have to get you out of the car. We can't just sit here. We might get hit again."

She unfastened his seat belt and reached across to open his door. It was stuck. She opened her own door and started to get out to go around, when Kyle's door was suddenly yanked open and Spence leaned down to gaze inside.

Natalie was almost glad to see him. Almost.

"I was right behind you," he said. "I saw the crash."

"I'm bleeding," Kyle said unnecessarily.

"So I see." Spence slipped his arms around the little boy and easily lifted him from the seat. "Looks like you're going to have quite a shiner there, too. Let's get you out of there, buddy, and have a look."

Natalie climbed out of the car and joined them at the side of the road. Spence had knelt and was cradling Kyle across his lap. "It's not that bad, but he probably needs stitches," he told Natalie. "We'd better get him to a hospital."

"What about the car? Should I just leave it?"

A couple of passersby had stopped to help. One of them said, "The other guy's long gone. He just high-tailed it out of here after he hit you. Probably a DWI."

"Call the police," Spence said. "When they get here, tell them they can find us at the hospital. Meanwhile, maybe a couple of you could push the car out of the street."

"Sure. But isn't it against the law to leave the scene of an accident?"

Spence stood, still holding Kyle in his arms. "You let me worry about that."

"WE WANT A PLASTIC surgeon," Spence said. Natalie just gazed at him in surprise. They were seated in an emergency-room cubicle, watching while a nurse and the resident on duty examined Kyle. Natalie had been so relieved to get him to the hospital that it had never even occurred to her to request a plastic surgeon.

The nurse glanced up. "I saw Dr. Redmond in the hallway a few minutes ago. He may still be here."

"Page him," Dr. Whitting said, obviously unfazed by Spence's request.

Within minutes the plastic surgeon had been summoned, and while he worked on Kyle, Spence and Natalie stood outside in the waiting room.

"What happened?" Spence asked, after Natalie had declined his offer of a cup of coffee.

"Didn't you see? Whoever hit us ran a red light," Natalie said. "I had a green light, and I was already in the intersection when the other car just came blazing through. I couldn't get out of the way in time."

Natalie shivered, thinking about the accident. Suddenly, the strange phone call she'd gotten earlier came rushing back to her. The gruff voice warning her, *"You know what I want. I want what's mine. Cooperate, and nobody else has to get hurt."*

And Anthony in a rage the night he'd been murdered: *"You thought you could pull a fast one on me, didn't you? You've always been just a little too clever for your own good, Natalie. But not this time. Now hand them over before I do something we might both regret."*

Natalie's heart thudded against her chest. What was going on here? Anthony had accused her of finding something that belonged to him. The voice on the phone accused her of having something that belonged to *him*. But what? What were they looking for? What had she inadvertently gotten herself involved in?

And what did it have to do with Anthony's murder?

"Natalie?" She jumped when Spence's hand touched her arm. He was gazing down at her strangely. "What's wrong?"

"I'm...not sure." She was on the verge of telling him about the phone call earlier when she stopped suddenly, realizing who he was. He was a Bishop. He believed she'd murdered his brother. How could she confide in him? How could she trust him?

But a little voice in the back of her mind reminded her that he was a seasoned professional, an FBI agent. If anyone would know what to do about the voice on the phone, about the accident, it was Spence.

Still, something held her back. An image of Irene at the cemetery threatening to take away her son. And

Spence had known about it. He'd known about it and he hadn't warned her. How could she trust him now? Supposing she confided in him and he ran straight to Irene? She could use this as ammunition in a custody fight. If she could prove Natalie couldn't take care of Kyle, or that Kyle was in danger because of her...

Another thought occurred to Natalie. What if the Bishops were behind all this? What if they had paid someone to call her earlier, and then hired that same someone to ram her car? She wouldn't put it past Irene or Anthea to do something that underhanded, and she knew exactly what Melinda was capable of. But what about Spence? How far would he be willing to go to prove his loyalty to his family? And why had he been following her from the cemetery? That seemed just a little too convenient to Natalie.

She opened her mouth to ask him about that, but just then the cubicle door opened and Dr. Redmond stepped out. He smiled at them both. "Mr. and Mrs. Bishop?"

Natalie started to correct him, but Spence spoke first. "How's Kyle?"

"He'll be fine. I'm recommending you keep him here overnight, though, just as a precaution. I've talked to Dr. Whitting and he agrees."

Fear knotted Natalie's stomach. "But I thought you said he was going to be fine."

The doctor turned to her. "He is. But he took a nasty bump on the head, and at his age, his condition should be closely monitored for the next several hours. I've already called upstairs and arranged a room."

"Can I see him?" Natalie asked, unable to keep the quiver of emotion out of her voice.

"Sure. Go on in. I've explained the situation to him, but I'm sure he'd like to hear it from you." Dr. Redmond placed a reassuring hand on Spence's shoulder. "Don't worry. We patched him up just fine. That's a real good-looking kid you got there."

"Thanks," Spence mumbled.

Natalie said nothing. She didn't dare.

Chapter Seven

"Mom, you didn't have to do that. He's only going to be in here overnight."

"I don't care," her mother said, placing the tiny Christmas tree on the nightstand beside Kyle's hospital bed and plugging in the lights. "When he wakes up, the first thing he'll see is his Christmas tree. That's bound to cheer him up."

Natalie stared down at her sleeping son. It was still early, but after Kyle had eaten his dinner, he'd fallen promptly asleep. She had been sitting by his bedside, watching him closely even though a nurse came in regularly to check on him.

"How's Dad?" she asked anxiously.

"Now don't you go worrying about him," her mother said, fussing with Kyle's bedcovers. "He's fine. He said to tell you he'll be by in the morning to pick us all up."

"But you don't have to spend the night," Natalie protested. Her mother had spent countless hours in the hospital when her father had his heart attack. Another night in a hospital room was probably the last place she wanted to be.

But she waved off Natalie's protest. "Do you honestly think I'm going to let my only grandson stay overnight in the hospital without me here to keep an eye on him? I'm staying, and that's final."

Natalie smiled, relieved in spite of herself. "Thanks, Mom. To tell you the truth, I could use the company right now. I've been sitting here thinking about how badly he could have been hurt...."

"But he wasn't. Concentrate on the positive," her mother told her. "Isn't that what I always taught you?"

Natalie nodded, trying to do as her mother instructed. She was right. The accident could have been a lot worse. Natalie had a lot to be grateful for, and she would do well to remember that in the trying times ahead.

But still...

She couldn't help thinking. She couldn't help worrying.

Her gaze returned to her son. The lights in the room had been dimmed, and the soft flash of the tiny Christmas-tree lights cast little dancing shadows across Kyle's sleeping face. "He really is beautiful, isn't he?" she said quietly, thinking that of all her blessings, he was her most precious.

"He's almost as beautiful as my own child." Her mother came around the bed and wrapped her arms around Natalie.

Natalie rested her head on her mother's shoulder. "I'm so scared," she whispered.

"I know. But everything's going to be okay. You'll see."

"You really believe that, don't you?"

"With all my heart."

Restless, Natalie walked over to the window to stare out at the parking lot. It was a clear night with a full moon and a light breeze that skimmed through the oasis of magnolia trees and azalea bushes planted in the center of the lot. The bushes were trimmed with little green lights that winked like fireflies in the darkness.

Natalie focused on one of the lights, thinking about the fullness of her life, about everything she had to be grateful for, and yet, like Gatsby staring at that green light across the water, she yearned for something that could never be.

"What is it, Natalie?"

She continued to stare at the light. "I'm just feeling a little down tonight and I can't seem to shake it."

"Is it something you want to talk about?"

Natalie hesitated, then shrugged. "I know you and Dad would never ask, but I want you to know something. I want you to hear it from me." She turned and faced her mother. "I didn't kill Anthony."

Her mother walked over and took Natalie's hands in hers. "Do you remember that time when you were nine, maybe ten years old and you found a squirrel on the side of the street that had been hit by a car? The poor little thing was still alive, but just barely. Without hesitation you took off your brand-new sweater and wrapped it around the squirrel's little body, then picked it up and carried it ten blocks to the vet. The squirrel died in your arms while you were sitting in the waiting room, and you cried all the way home. You told me later that you knew the exact moment when the poor little thing's heart stopped beating, and it was as if a part of you had died, too. Do you remember that?"

Natalie nodded.

Her mother put her hands up to the sides of Natalie's face. "Do you think for one moment, for even one second, that I could ever believe that same sweet, sensitive girl could ever take another life? Why, I'd sooner believe it about myself."

A tear spilled over and ran down Natalie's cheek.

SPENCE STOOD IN THE HALL, listening to that quiet, melodious voice comforting Natalie. He closed his eyes for a moment, wondering what it would be like to have that kind of unconditional love and support, the kind of blind faith Joy Silver had in her daughter.

He thought back to his conversation yesterday with his own mother. After more than ten years of estrangement, Irene had finally asked him to come home. But not because she wanted his comfort or support. Not because she loved him or needed him, but because she wanted him to help her exact her revenge. Irene wanted him to help her punish the woman who had taken away her other son, the only son she had ever cared about.

Spence told himself it didn't matter anymore. He'd come to terms with all that years ago. He didn't need anyone. In fact, in his line of work, it was better to be able to pick up and leave at a moment's notice, leaving no one or nothing of importance behind. In his line of work, a family made you vulnerable. Made you care too much.

Or so he'd always told himself.

But looking at Natalie and her mother now was like staring into a looking glass and glimpsing a whole new world. A foreign world. A world in which people actually cared whether you lived or died, and suddenly Spence wondered what his own life might have been like if he'd had that same kind of love and devotion. That same kind of blind faith.

Would he have been a kinder man? A happier man? Would he still have chosen the same profession? A profession that often led him into the darkest, seediest corners of humanity. A profession that sometimes demanded the cruelest of sacrifices. A profession that had irrevocably changed him over the years, turned him into the steely-eyed stranger that stared back at him from the mirror every morning and every night; a man who had been willing to betray his own brother in the name of justice, because fighting for justice was the only thing that gave his life meaning.

He gazed around the hospital room, his eyes resting on the tiny Christmas tree, a scrawny affair with branches barely able to support a single string of colored lights, and yet, at that moment, it seemed to symbolize so much that had always been missing from his life. Love, hope, joy. And peace. He couldn't remember a time when he'd known any peace in his life, except maybe for seven years ago, very briefly, when he'd met Natalie. When he had fallen in love with her.

But that was before he'd gone away.

That was before she'd married Anthony and had a child with him.

Of all the things that Anthony had been given in his lifetime, of all the riches he'd possessed, there had only been one thing that Spence had ever really coveted. He'd taken some measure of satisfaction in that knowledge. But as he gazed at Anthony's sleeping son, he suddenly realized with a pang of guilt that now there were two.

You're getting maudlin, he told himself grimly. *As bad as an old woman.*

The spirit of the season was obviously getting to him in a way it never had before, and that wouldn't do. He was here in San Antonio to do a job, and it was time to get on with it.

He looked down at the stuffed bear he'd picked up in the hospital gift shop. Purely an impulse purchase, because the Santa Claus hat perched on the bear's pudgy head had caught his eye. But Kyle was probably too old for stuffed animals.

Showed how much he knew about kids, Spence thought. Better stick to the things he did know about. Like looking for lost diamonds. And putting murderers away for life.

He turned away, looking for a trash can.

NATALIE STOOD IN THE hallway and gazed at the man walking toward the nurse's station. She thought she'd glimpsed Spence in the doorway of Kyle's room a second ago, but before she could say anything, he'd turned and walked away.

Surely it wasn't him. Why would he have come back? After Kyle had been moved upstairs earlier, it had seemed to Natalie that Spence couldn't wait to get away from them.

She'd told herself that was fine by her. He'd bailed her out of jail and she was grateful to him for that, although she still suspected he had an ulterior motive. She was also grateful that he'd helped her with Kyle this afternoon after the accident and had run interference for her with the police. She appreciated everything he'd done, but anything beyond gratitude was treading on dangerous ground. Anything remotely resembling attraction was asking for trouble.

The kind of trouble Natalie didn't want or need.

Unfortunately, it was the kind of trouble one rarely had control over. She'd known it the moment she'd seen him standing in the doorway of the interrogation room, his eyes dark with suspicion and accusation and maybe even hate. She'd known then, as she knew now, that what she had once felt for Spencer Bishop had never really died.

God, help me, she thought. *How can I be so stupid? So weak? He's a Bishop, for God's sake. Anthony's brother. A man you had little more than a one-night stand with. There is nothing there. There never was. You were young and stupid and impressionable. And Spence was...*

She closed her eyes, remembering.

Spence had been young, too. And handsome. A dark and brooding FBI agent with an inner intensity that had frightened her at first. And then thrilled her.

It had been raining the day they first met, and Natalie was feeling bluer than usual. Her parents had been gone several months by that time, and she was having trouble adjusting to a new college.

Spence had seemed to sense her loneliness, and at first, she'd thought it was because he was lonely, too. Later, of course, she realized that he was simply an expert at reading people. It was all a part of his job.

But that first day, when he'd walked over to her, leaned across her desk, and whispered to her that it was his birthday and he didn't want to spend it alone, Natalie didn't have it in her heart to resist. No one should spend a birthday alone.

So they made arrangements for him to pick her up after work, and then went to dinner at a quaint, candlelit restaurant off the beaten track. They talked some, but not a lot because both of them were introverts and a little uneasy about the developing attraction between them.

Afterward, they strolled along the Riverwalk, and Spence kissed her in a secluded corner beneath a bridge, with mariachi music playing in the background and a fountain splashing nearby. Then he asked her to come back to his hotel room with him, but Natalie shyly refused. That night.

The following week they were together constantly. He picked her up daily from work and they went out to dinner or to a movie or sometimes for a walk. They kissed and touched—their attraction was simmering by this time—but always Natalie managed to keep her senses under control. Until that last night, when Spence told her he'd been called back to Washington and they wouldn't be able to see each other for a while.

That night Natalie invited him back to her apartment, and he stayed until the wee hours of the morning. They had one glorious, passion-filled night, and then he was gone.

He didn't come back to San Antonio for almost two months, during which time Natalie had no phone calls and no letters from him. During which time, doubts and fear besieged her.

During which time, Anthony began to pursue her.

Smooth, suave, aristocratic Anthony, who told Natalie all about his little brother—how Spence made a habit of using women, then throwing them away like so much garbage. How Spence had never cared about anyone but himself. How he already had a fiancée in Washington, and that was why he'd rushed back at a moment's notice.

Anthony even showed Natalie pictures taken in Washington of Spence and a gorgeous, sophisticated-looking woman who obviously adored him, and Natalie had burned with anger and humiliation. How had she allowed herself to succumb so easily to his seduction? Why had she believed him when he'd told her that he'd never felt this way about another woman?

It was the oldest line in the book, and Natalie had fallen for it so easily, when, in reality, she had been nothing more to Spencer Bishop than a new conquest—someone he wanted to sleep with, but certainly not the kind of woman he wanted to marry.

And through it all, Anthony had been there to hold her hand, to tell her that she *was* special, and that his brother was a fool. Any man would be proud to have a woman like Natalie for his wife. Any man would want to take care of her, have a family with her.

If Natalie would just trust him, he would help her out of a desperate situation. He would love, honor, and cherish her in a way his brother never could.

By the time Spence returned to San Antonio, Natalie and Anthony were married. And even in that short period of time, she'd already realized what a horrible mistake she'd made, what kind of man her husband really was. Which had made her wonder if he'd lied to her about Spence, but by then, it was too late. She'd already struck a bargain with Anthony, and there was no going back.

As all those memories rushed through her, Natalie hesitated in the hallway, wondering if she should call out to Spence. Or if she should let him go.

But he seemed to have sensed her intense scrutiny. He stopped and turned to glance over his shoulder. When he saw her, something flashed in his green eyes—a look Natalie couldn't quite define. For a moment, she wondered if he had been thinking about the past, too. About the night that had seemed so right . . . so inevitable.

The night that had changed her life forever.

He turned slowly and started walking back toward her. Natalie's pulse raced as she stared up at him, taking in in a heartbeat the dark expression on his face, the glimpse of secrets in his eyes . . . so dangerous and yet so irresistible.

How had her life come back to this? she wondered with a sinking feeling in her stomach. How had she managed to come full circle in seven years? Anthony Bishop was still controlling her life, even from his grave, and Spence . . . Spence was still making her want what she knew she couldn't have.

In seven years she'd learned nothing.

In seven years, she was still weak and vulnerable where Spencer Bishop was concerned.

But now she had her son to think about, she told herself firmly. Now she had Kyle to protect.

"How is he?" Spence asked, as if reading her thoughts. He stopped directly in front of her, so that she had to look up at him. How like a Bishop, she reflected.

She stepped back and crossed her arms as she leaned against the wall, taking away some of his advantage. "He's fine. I didn't expect to see you again tonight." Her gaze dropped to the stuffed bear he held in one hand, and for some insane reason, she felt her throat knot.

What was the matter with her, for God's sake? She hadn't broken down when she'd been arrested for Anthony's murder, and she hadn't fallen apart after the car accident and Kyle's session with the plastic surgeon. So why did the sight of Spencer Bishop clutching a teddy bear he'd bought for Kyle make her want to weep uncontrollably?

Seeing the direction of her stare, Spence held up the bear and looked at it for a moment as though he hadn't a clue how he came to be holding it. Then he shrugged. "I bought this for Kyle...saw it in the gift shop.... But I guess...he's probably too old for stuffed toys."

"No, he's not," Natalie said quietly. "He'll love it."

With another shrug, Spence held it out to her. She raised her eyebrows. "Don't you want to give it to him yourself?"

"I thought he was sleeping."

"He is, but the nurses come to check on him every so often. They have to wake him to make sure he's... okay."

"He is, isn't he?"

Natalie smiled. "Yes. He's tough. Takes more than a bump on the head to slow him down."

Spence laughed softly, and Natalie realized with a start that she'd never heard him laugh before. Not once. And that fact struck her as being incredibly sad.

Don't, she warned herself. *Don't feel sorry for Spencer Bishop.*

If he lived in a world without laughter, it was because he chose to. Chose to retreat into his own cold, dark, unreachable place. A place of lies and deceit. A world that had once sucked Natalie in, and then almost destroyed her.

She pushed her hair back with one hand as she gazed up at him, her sadness and sympathy gone. Her eyes, she knew, mirrored the suspicion and distrust she saw in his. "Why did you really come back here, Spence? I don't think it was to see Kyle."

He hesitated for a moment, then said, "You're right. I wanted to talk to you."

"About?"

"Everything."

"That's a broad topic," she said, straightening away from the wall. She glanced around, wondering what people might think if they saw them together and recognized them—the woman accused of murdering Anthony Bishop, and Anthony Bishop's brother, the man who had bailed her out of jail. The man who had once been her lover, one night long ago.

"I want to ask you some questions about the night Anthony died," Spence said.

"Why?"

"Because there are a few things I'd like to clear up."

"It's all in the police report."

"Maybe. But I'd rather hear it from you."

Natalie removed her glasses and rubbed her eyes. "I've been through it so many times. It's a nightmare. I can't bear to repeat it again. Not now. Not with my son lying in there hurt because..."

"Because?" Spence's eyes darkened. "What were you about to say, Natalie?"

"Nothing," she mumbled, still unable to bring herself to trust him. She slipped her glasses back on, as if they somehow gave her courage. "Only that...I had so much on my mind today, I might not have been paying enough attention to my driving. I might have avoided that accident."

"I don't think so. You were already in the intersection when the other car ran the red light. There was nothing you could have done."

"Maybe not." But she still wasn't convinced. The voice on the telephone earlier had implied a threat when he'd told her he knew where her son was. What if that car had deliberately hit them, because someone wanted something Natalie had? Except she had no idea what it was.

Tell him, she ordered herself. *Tell him and demand police protection for Kyle.* While another voice whispered through her mind, *Anything you say can and will be used against you in a court of law.*

But it wasn't the murder trial she was worried about now. It was the custody battle with Irene that made her turn away from Spence in order to hide the fear in her eyes.

"There's nothing more I can tell you," she said. "About anything."

"Oh, I think there is."

Natalie started to protest, but just then her mother popped her head around the door. "Natalie? Kyle's awake. He's asking for you, honey."

"I'll be right there." She turned back to Spence, hoping to end the conversation then and there, but to her chagrin, she heard her mother say, "Why, hello again. It's Spence, isn't it?"

"Mrs. Silver. Nice to see you again."

"Joy, please. I'm not one to stand on ceremony." Her eyes lit on the bear in Spence's hand. "Oh, how adorable! Did you bring it for Kyle? Well, then, you have to come in, so he can thank you."

Natalie went quickly to her son's bedside, and bent to kiss him on each cheek and then lightly on his bandaged forehead. "How are you feeling, sweetie?"

"Good," he said. "I'm thirsty."

Natalie poured him a glass of water from the pitcher on the nightstand. Kyle's eyes widened when he saw the tree for the first time. "Awesome! Where did that come from?"

"From Santa, who else?" his grandmother piped in. She was standing on the other side of the bed and she winked at Kyle, then patted his little arm. "He couldn't let you stay in here without a Christmas tree, now could he? That wouldn't seem like Christmas at all. And speaking of Christmas, look who's brought you a present."

As if on cue, Kyle's gaze turned to the foot of his bed, where Spence had just stepped into the room. "Hi," Kyle said.

"Hey, there." Spence looked decidedly uncomfortable, as if he didn't quite know what to do or say. Then he held the bear out to Kyle and said apologetically, "I hope this is okay. I guess I don't know much about what six-year-old boys are into these days."

"Wow! You bought this for me? Thanks!" Kyle exclaimed, as if a stuffed bear wearing a Santa Claus hat was the one present he'd been waiting his whole life for. Natalie could have kissed him, especially when she saw the spark of pleasure in Spence's eyes.

"You're welcome," he said, smiling at Kyle in a way Natalie had never seen him smile before. That smile made her heart do funny things inside her chest.

"I see I was right," Spence said. "You've got yourself quite a shiner."

"Really?" Kyle perked right up at the thought of a black eye. "Can I see?"

Shaking her head, Natalie handed him a mirror.

"Whoa, dude," Kyle exclaimed, obviously quite impressed with his bruised and battered reflection. "I never had a black eye before."

"Yes, you have," Natalie corrected him. "When you were only a year old. You fell off the dining-room table. How you managed to get up there, I never quite figured out."

Her mother laughed. "I remember you writing to me about that. And then there was the time when he was three, and your father and I were home that one summer. Dad took him to a company softball game. Poor little thing got hit right in the eye with a foul ball. Dad felt terrible."

"How come I don't remember any of this?" Kyle demanded.

"Because you were too small," Natalie said.

"So why didn't you tell me?"

"I didn't know it was something you'd want to know. Silly me, I didn't realize black eyes were so important."

"Sure, they are," Spence said. "Just like bikes without training wheels and real baseball bats, not plastic ones, and really gross skinned knees. Right?"

Kyle nodded, terribly pleased that someone understood him, and that that someone was a man. Male bonding was a concept Natalie tried not to think about too much. She was a single mother raising her son the best way she knew how. Surely she couldn't be faulted for that.

But Kyle missed having a man in his life. Natalie had always known that, but there wasn't much she could do about it. Anthony hadn't been in the picture until a few weeks before he died, and even then, only at his own convenience. Natalie's father had been out of the country off and on for the last seven years or so, and there hadn't been any other men in her life to speak of. No wonder Kyle seemed so taken with Spence.

Or at least, that was what Natalie told herself. She couldn't let herself believe it was anything more—that Kyle and Spence shared any kind of bond, other than a last name and a somewhat vague physical resemblance. They both had the Bishop eyes. But then, so had Anthony.

Natalie glanced down at her son, who was contentedly playing with his bear. Spence and her mother had moved away from the bed and were talking in low tones. Natalie heard her mother say, "...needs to get out of here for a while. Would you mind taking her out to dinner?"

Natalie was horrified. Her mother was arranging for her to spend time with a Bishop. Spencer Bishop. She was actually asking him to take her poor, pitiful daughter out to dinner.

Heat crept up her neck and spread across her face. What was her mother thinking? But, of course, she knew nothing of Spence and Natalie's background, their brief interlude. She only knew that he was Anthony's brother and that he had bailed her daughter out of jail. Because of the latter, Joy seemed perfectly willing to overlook the former.

But Natalie wasn't.

She said, "I'm fine, Mom. I don't want to leave right now."

But her mother had that look on her face—the one that clearly said, *I'm your mother. I know best, so don't argue.*

"You've been cooped up in this hospital room all afternoon and evening, and this morning you were cooped up at home. Before that you were in that awful place—" She stopped herself, staring down at Kyle's wide green eyes, bright and alert and taking in her every word. "All I'm saying is that a little fresh air and a hot meal would do you a world of good."

Before Natalie could offer another protest, Spence said, "She's right. It would do you good to get out for a while."

Natalie had no desire to spend the evening with Spencer Bishop, but unfortunately, everyone seemed to be conspiring against her. Even her own son. "I don't mind, Mom. Honest. Gram can tell me a story while you're gone."

"Ah, yes," his grandmother said, coming to stand beside Kyle's bed. "I believe we did leave our starship captain stranded on that dismal little planet in the Chymmyrian galaxy, didn't we?"

Kyle nodded eagerly. "He lost his phaser."

"And his communicator," his grandmother said. "Well, things did, indeed, look dire for Captain Killian...."

Out in the hall, Natalie hesitated, gazing up at Spence. "Look...you really don't have to be railroaded into doing this. I can just go down to the cafeteria and grab a bite to eat."

"I'd really like to take you to dinner."

"Why? So you can grill me some more?" She had no delusions about his intentions.

His eyes darkened for a moment at her deliberate provocation. Then he shrugged and said, "No. So we can talk. That's something you and I have never done much of, is it, Natalie?"

Chapter Eight

Natalie's trepidation steadily mounted as Spence headed downtown, found a public parking area, and pulled his car into a space. He cut the engine and turned to her, his arm resting lightly along the back of her seat. Natalie didn't know why, but she was acutely aware of his hand so close to her hair, of having his face mere inches from hers in the small confines of the car.

In the light from the street, she could see his eyes—dark and shadowy—studying her intently and she grew even more nervous. He said something, and the movement of his lips drew her gaze like a moth to flame, irresistibly attracted to danger.

"So you don't mind?" he was saying.

"Mind?" Reluctantly she lifted her gaze to meet his questioning eyes.

"That I brought you here."

She shrugged. "Why should I mind? I love the Riverwalk. My shop's located here."

"I know."

"But how—"

"I was there the night Anthony was murdered," he said and got out of the car.

Natalie had no choice but to follow. She joined him at the top of the steps, and together they descended to the river level. It was still fairly early and the stores were buzzing with shoppers, the restaurants and bistros spilling over with music and laughter.

Luminarias glowed softly along the sidewalks, while thousands and thousands of colored lights hung in streamers from the huge trees lining the river. Against the dark green surface of the water, the glistening lights sparkled like jewels.

It was a fairyland, a place of enchantment, and Natalie suddenly felt as though she had stepped through a wardrobe into a world where everything might not be as it seemed. Where danger and darkness might well be disguised by the beauty and magic of the moment.

Spence took her elbow and guided her through the maze of tables hugging the banks of the river, and the throng of tourists and revelers strolling along the sidewalk. Finally he stopped in front of her own building, and Natalie's eyes were drawn upward.

On the top level, light shone from Blanche's windows proclaiming her shop open for business, while on the bottom level, Delmontico's drew a brisk dinner crowd. But in between, on the second level, the windows of Silver Bells remained ominously dark, and although she couldn't see it, Natalie knew the yellow police tape stamped "Crime Scene" would still be barricading her door. She turned away, saddened by the sight and the memories.

"I've heard good things about this restaurant," Spence said. "But if you don't want to stay, we can go somewhere else."

"No, it's fine." Natalie gazed around, looking everywhere but at the second story. She couldn't avoid it forever, though. This moment was bound to happen, and she might as well get it over with.

Sooner or later, she would have to come back here and reopen her shop. She would have to find a way to deal with the memories of that night and move on, because she still had a business to run, she still had a child to support, and she still had a life to live. She couldn't hide in Narnia forever.

Frank Delmontico saw them and wove his way through the tables. He was not a tall man—five seven or so, only a couple of inches taller than Natalie. But he was toughly built, his arms and shoulders powerful looking beneath the loose white shirt he wore. His black hair was slicked straight back, highlighting his dark, fathomless eyes and his swarthy complexion.

When Natalie introduced him to Spence, something flashed in those dark eyes, a wariness that vanished almost instantly. Then he turned on his heel and led them to a candlelit table near the river.

It was a warm night, but the breeze off the water was chilly. Natalie wrapped her light jacket around her shoulders and shivered as they sat down.

"Would you rather eat inside?" Spence asked.

"No, I like it out here. I love looking at all the lights. It's so beautiful. I never get tired of this place. Every season brings its own magic."

"I've missed San Antonio," Spence said unexpectedly, after a waiter had come by to take their drink order. "When I left Washington, it was bitterly cold and pouring rain. Very depressing."

"No snow?"

"Not yet, but there were predictions for Christmas."

Natalie's gaze scanned the water, fastened on a barge outlined in lights carrying a group of loud tourists downriver. "As much as I love this warm weather, sometimes I think it would be nice to have snow for the holidays. I've never had a white Christmas."

"In San Antonio that would take a miracle."

"I'm not sure I believe in miracles anymore," Natalie said softly, her voice full of regret.

"I don't think I ever did. Miracles are for fairy tales and dreams. In the real world, if you want something badly enough, you have to make it happen. You can't just sit around waiting for it to snow."

She glanced up sharply. His eyes, dark and seductive, stared back at her, and Natalie felt something tremble inside her. "But some things are beyond our control."

"And some things aren't." He leaned toward her across the table. Candlelight flashed in his eyes. "Do you want to find out what really happened to Anthony?"

She looked at him in shock. "Of course, I do. But I thought you were convinced . . . of my guilt."

"Do you really think I would have bailed you out of jail if I thought you killed my brother?"

The breeze picked up and the candle flickered wildly between them. His eyes deepened mysteriously. What was he really saying? Natalie wondered. Did he really believe in her innocence? Or, as before, years ago, was he merely telling her what he knew she wanted to hear? Was he playing on her emotions to get what he wanted?

The question was, what exactly did he want this time?

"What did you have in mind?" Natalie asked suspiciously.

"I'd like to help you get to the bottom of this mystery. I'd like to help you find the real killer."

"I never said I was looking for the killer," she said quickly, her heart bouncing off the wall of her chest. She wasn't a detective, for God's sake.

Spence sat back in his chair and studied the candle flame. "I've had some experience in dealing with local law enforcement. Once they have their suspect in custody, their investigation is pretty much over."

"Are you saying that since they believe I'm guilty, they won't even look for anyone else?"

"That's what I'm saying, Natalie."

"Then I could go to jail," she whispered in horror. "I could be convicted of a crime I didn't commit."

"It's possible. A lot of innocent people are in prison. More than you imagine."

Images flashed through her mind. Dark, dreary cells. Endless hours crawling by. And the loneliness, the sheer helplessness ...

Natalie suddenly felt sick at her stomach. "Why would you want to help me?"

Spence lifted the drink the waiter put in front of him. "Anthony was my brother. We had our differences, but he was still my brother. My own flesh and blood. And somewhere out there, his killer roams free. Anthony may not be his last victim."

Cooperate, and no one else has to get hurt.

"How do you know it's a man?" Natalie asked. "Anthony had a lot of enemies. Many of them were probably women." She was thinking of one in particular. He'd been about to divorce Melinda and not give her a cent. Texas was a community-property state, but Natalie knew her ex-husband had been expert in finding ways around the law when it suited him.

"Who, specifically, are you talking about?"

"Kyle overheard Anthony telling Melinda he wanted a divorce. He was going to cut her off without a penny."

Spence's brows rose. "Kyle said this?"

Natalie nodded. "In fact, he recorded their conversation."

This seemed to interest Spence a great deal. He leaned forward again. "Does he still have the tape?"

"I don't know. He claims to have lost the recorder."

"Claims?"

Natalie toyed with her own drink, a glass of red wine. "Kyle has a habit of hiding things—for safekeeping, he says—then forgetting where he put them."

"I'd like to talk to him," Spence said.

"Not now. He's been through too much. Maybe in a few days—"

"In a few days, the trail will only grow colder. We have to move fast."

He *was* moving fast. Too fast to suit Natalie. She hadn't agreed to work with him. She still wasn't sure she even trusted him.

"Kyle doesn't know anything about the murder," she said angrily. "He's just a little boy."

"I would never say or do anything to hurt him."

Their eyes met over the candle flame. Natalie wanted to deny the quiver in her stomach, the shiver of nerves along her spine, but she couldn't. Not with the way he was suddenly looking at her.

She forced her gaze away. "I thought we came here to eat," she said. "So let's order. I need to get back to the hospital."

For the next several minutes, after they'd placed their orders and waited for their food to arrive, they turned their talk from murder. Natalie asked him about his work in Washington, and he asked her about her shop.

"A Christmas store," he said. "That suits you."

Natalie laughed softly. "You might even say it was inevitable, since I was born on Christmas Eve."

"I didn't know that."

There were a lot of things about her he didn't know. It was ironic, she thought. He'd been her lover, and yet he didn't even know the date of her birth. He hadn't even asked. Hadn't cared enough, she realized now.

"My birthday's in November," he commented, making small talk.

"November 16th," she said, before thinking.

"So you remembered." His gaze met hers.

She tried to laugh lightly. "I remember that you're a Scorpio. Dark, brooding, intense. And secretive," she couldn't resist adding. "Anthony was a Gemini. Dual personalities."

"So what are you?"

"Capricorn. Impulsive. Easily fooled."

"And Kyle?"

Natalie studied her wineglass. "A Leo. Powerful, commanding, kinglike. He loves that one."

"When is his birthday?"

Natalie glanced up. "You . . . don't know?"

"I never asked."

Never cared enough to, she thought again. The knowledge hurt her, although she knew it shouldn't. Spence hadn't married his fiancée, the woman Anthony had shown her in the picture, and Natalie had never asked why. She liked to think it was because she hadn't cared enough, either.

"I didn't keep in touch with my family back then," Spence was saying. "In fact, two days ago, when I went over to tell my mother that Anthony was dead, was the first time I'd talked to her in years."

Just then, the waiter brought their dinners, and Natalie was saved from having to respond. She thought about Spence's estrangement from his family. In the year that Anthony and Natalie had been married, she hadn't been around Irene Bishop that much. The older woman's open disapproval was like the thrust of a knife blade. Natalie had avoided her whenever possible, but even during the few brief audiences Irene had granted to her, Natalie had discerned very quickly that Anthony was the favorite, and that the worth of Irene's other children was measured by their devotion to him.

In spite of herself, Natalie felt a stab of sympathy for Spence. Her own parents had adored her from the moment she was born, and they'd let her know every day of her life how wonderful she was, what a precious gift she was to them.

Having been surrounded by their love, Natalie couldn't imagine what it must have been like for Spence, growing up in that cold mausoleum of a home with an even colder mother, a father who ignored him, and a sister and brother who despised him.

Unlike her own magical youth, Spence's childhood had been a cold, barren wasteland—a place where it was always winter but never Christmas.

They finished eating in silence. While Spence settled the check, Natalie got up and walked to the water's edge, staring at the dazzling reflection of lights. Sensing a presence behind her, she turned to find Frank Delmontico watching her.

Even though she and Blanche had eaten here often, Frank had always kept his distance, treating them as he would any other customers, always careful to foster nothing more than a nodding acquaintance. His intense scrutiny now made her uneasy. She wondered if he, like everyone else, was now looking at her in a new light, thinking that all these years he'd been located downstairs from a cold-blooded killer.

Rather than turning away when he saw that she'd caught him staring, he walked over to her. The full sleeves of his white shirt billowed softly in the breeze.

He came right to the point. "That man with you. He's a cop, right?"

"FBI," Natalie said, glancing back at their table.

Frank's eyes darkened. "Why is a federal agent working on a simple murder case?"

Natalie had no idea why Frank Delmontico had taken such a sudden interest in her, but she saw no harm in answering him. She shrugged and said, "He's not officially on the case. Anthony Bishop was his brother."

Frank showed not the slightest hint of surprise. He turned and his gaze followed Natalie's to their table, where Spence waited for his credit card to be returned. He looked up and his gaze met Natalie's briefly before narrowing on Frank.

"I can see the resemblance," Frank muttered. He shook his head, turning away. "Anthony Bishop's brother an FBI agent. Who would have thought that?"

Natalie stared at him in surprise. "You *knew* Anthony?"

"Only by reputation," Frank was quick to amend. "We had a mutual acquaintance."

Before she could ask him who that acquaintance might be, Frank leaned toward her. His voice lowered ominously. "Your ex-husband was into some dirty business, Natalie. I'd hate to see you get drawn into something you can't handle."

"What kind of dirty business?" she asked quickly.

"Dealings with the underworld," Frank said. "Anthony Bishop had his fingers in a lot of pies."

"Do you know something about his murder?"

"I don't know anything," Frank replied. "But I hear things. And the word on the street is, you could be in a lot of trouble."

"With whom?"

He shrugged, obviously having said all he intended to.

"I've been accused of Anthony's murder," she said desperately. "If you know something that could help clear my name, please tell me."

"Just be careful," Frank said. "Be careful who you trust."

He stared over her shoulder, and Natalie glanced behind to see that Spence had left their table and was walking toward them.

She turned back to Frank, but he had already melted into the shadows near the restaurant.

"WHAT DID HE WANT?" Spence asked.

"I'm not sure. He...warned me."

"About what?"

"About you, I think." She looked up to find Spence staring down at her, his gaze hard, suspicious.

"And what did you say?"

"I didn't say anything, but I can take care of myself. I know better than to trust the wrong people."

"Do you?" They walked in silence for a moment, then he asked suddenly, "How long have you known Frank Delmontico?"

"Five years. He was already in the building when I opened my store. Why?"

Spence shrugged. "He looks familiar to me."

"You said you were here before...right after Anthony's...death. Maybe you saw him then."

Spence shook his head. "It was too early in the morning for the restaurants and shops to be open. I know I've seen him somewhere before, though. Sooner or later, it'll come to me." He paused for a moment, as if in deep concentration, then asked, "Who owns the store on the top level?"

"Blanche Jones. She's a good friend of mine."

"We might want to come back and talk to both of them. Find out if either of them saw or heard anything unusual the night of the murder."

"The police have already questioned them both," Natalie said. "I talked to Blanche the day after it happened." Blanche had been very distraught to learn that Natalie had been arrested for Anthony's murder. She'd been so upset, in fact, that she could hardly talk at first. Finally, she'd settled down and told Natalie that the police had been around, asking a lot of questions. Unfortunately, Blanche had closed early that night and had been home at the time of the murder. She hadn't seen or heard anything that could help Natalie. As for Frank, Blanche couldn't say.

"The police might not have asked the right questions," Spence said. "Tomorrow, I think we should come back and talk to them."

Natalie didn't point out that she hadn't agreed to work with him. But he'd frightened her with what he'd told her earlier about the investigation coming to a halt because the police had their suspect. If they weren't looking for the real killer, then who would?

At least Spence was a professional, an FBI agent. Who better to have helping her?

Someone you can trust, a little voice reminded her.

Unfortunately, no one filled that bill at the moment.

She sighed wearily. "All right. I guess it won't hurt to talk to them."

Another uneasy silence fell between them. They strolled along the Riverwalk, and Natalie tried very hard not to remember the last time they'd walked here together. But Spence's presence was making it difficult. He wasn't touching her, but she couldn't help remembering when he once had. He wasn't looking at her, but she couldn't stop thinking about the way he used to.

At the bottom of the steps that would take them to the street level and the parking lot where they'd left his car, Spence stopped and gazed down at her. Behind them the music and laughter faded away. The Christmas lights seemed to dim, and the only thing Natalie was aware of was the way his eyes deepened, and the way his lips opened, and the way her heart pounded inside her.

For a split second—an eternity—no one said anything. Then, very softly, Spence said, "Why did you marry him?"

He was still gazing down at her, and Natalie's breath caught in her throat. It was seven years too late to be having this conversation. Too late to change anything. But she found herself answering him anyway. "I married him because he was here and you weren't."

"As simple as that?" His voice turned bitter.

"No." She glanced away from those probing eyes. "There wasn't anything simple about it."

"Did you love him?"

"No."

Her blunt answer seemed to surprise him. "Then I repeat, why did you marry him?"

To get back at you, Natalie thought. *To prove to you that I was better than a one-night stand and to prove to myself that someone else wanted me, even if you didn't.*

And because she'd been nineteen, and pregnant, with nowhere else to turn.

Natalie had always wondered how differently things might have worked out if her parents hadn't been out of the country back then—if she'd had their love and wisdom to rely on. But as it was, she'd had no one. And the shame and embarrassment of what she'd done had made her unable to confide in her mother by letter or over the telephone. She knew her parents would have been devastated, and her father would have turned down an important promotion—an opportunity he'd worked for all his life—just to come home and be with her.

And Anthony had been there—an older man guiding her, protecting her, providing her with a solution that seemed to be the best for everyone. At that time, Natalie had no idea that he had his own hidden agenda, his own secret reasons for wanting to marry her.

"Why, Natalie?"

She sighed, trying to diminish the painful memories. "What difference does it make? It was all a long time ago. Anthony's dead and—"

"You and I are still here."

"So?"

The breeze loosened her hair, and automatically he reached up to smooth back the stray lock, then trailed the back of his hand down the side of her face.

And everything stilled within her.

"You still feel it, don't you?"

"No!"

He smiled slightly. "So emphatic. You didn't even have to ask what I was talking about. You know why? Because you do still feel it. It's still there."

"I don't know what you're talking about," she insisted, her nerve endings dancing along her spine.

"Then let me explain."

Before Natalie had time to turn away, before she even had time to catch her breath, he reached out to remove her glasses. His mouth lowered to hers.

And seven years vanished.

The moment his lips touched hers, she was once again that lonely, vulnerable nineteen-year-old and he was . . . Spence. A brooding, complex man who stirred powerful emotions inside her. A man who had always made her tremble at his nearness. A man who made her want nothing more than to be the one to turn on the light in his cold, dark, dismal world.

The kiss was surprisingly gentle. No demands, no recriminations, and for the moment, no regrets. Just a soft melting of souls as his fingers wove through her hair and his lips moved against hers.

A thousand emotions raced through Natalie. She'd forgotten this side of him. The tender, warm, caring side that, with just one kiss, could somehow bring her to her knees.

She wanted to slip her arms around his waist and hold him close. She wanted to tell him how many times over the years she'd dreamed of this moment. She wanted to share with him her most precious of secrets.

But she did none of that. Because even with his lips pressing against hers, even with his heart hammering beneath her splayed hand on his chest, she knew that all of this was a lie. Spencer Bishop was a lie. A chameleon as talented and ruthless as his brother. A man who was not what he seemed. A man of secrets...

She pulled away and he let her go. Her fingertips trembled against her lips as she gazed up at him. "Why did you do that?" she whispered.

"To prove a point."

"As simple as that?" she asked, using his own bitter words. She almost expected him to come back with hers. *Nothing about it was simple.* The kiss had undoubtedly complicated their already complex lives.

But Spence simply shrugged, his shoulders lifting slightly beneath the black leather jacket he wore. "As simple as that." His eyes never wavered from hers. "At least now we know what we're dealing with."

He said it so matter-of-factly, he might have been talking about a case instead of a kiss. Natalie didn't know why his tone suddenly angered her. "And what is that?"

"For a smart woman, you can certainly act dense when it suits you."

Her anger blossomed, mercifully dimming the other emotions storming through her. "I've made too many stupid mistakes in my life to ever claim to be smart. Letting you kiss me just now was one of them."

"Why?"

"Because—" Because it had stirred to life emotions that were best left dead. Because it had made her feel weak and vulnerable when she needed to be strong and invincible.

He'd trapped her and he knew it. His green eyes gleamed in the moonlight. "Because you know I'm right," he said softly. "The attraction is still there."

"Yes, it's still there," she acknowledged, lifting her chin in a tiny act of defiance. "But I don't want it to be."

He reached out and slipped her glasses back on her. The act was oddly gentle, belying the darkness in his eyes. "We don't always get what we want, Natalie. Haven't you learned that by now?"

SINCE THEY'D BEEN GONE longer than Natalie had meant to be, she called the hospital from Spence's cellular phone. Her mother answered and assured her Kyle was fine. Natalie could hear murmuring in the background, then her mother said, "There is just one tiny problem." Kyle's voice rose in distress, but Natalie couldn't make out what he was saying. "He wants to talk to you."

When Kyle got on the phone, Natalie asked quickly, "What's wrong, honey?"

"It's Fred."

"Fred? What about him?"

"I forgot to feed him before I left, and now Grandma says I can't go home till morning. He'll starve to death."

"No, he won't. He'll be fine until we get home. Turtles don't need much food."

"Fred does. And besides, you always say I'll get sick if I don't eat right. I don't want Fred to get sick. You have to go feed him, Mom. You just have to."

"Honey, Fred will be fine—"

"Please, Mom. If he gets sick . . ."

Natalie winced. If Fred got sick, Kyle would never forgive her. He thought the world of that turtle, ever since he'd rescued it from a drainage ditch after a rainstorm one day.

She sighed. "All right, I'll go feed Fred, if it'll make you feel better. But you have to promise me you'll try to get some sleep. That's the deal."

"I promise," Kyle said, smothering a yawn. It seemed she'd said the magic words.

She hung up and glanced at Spence. "Do you mind? Kyle insists that I go home and feed his turtle before coming back to the hospital. I know he won't get a bit of rest if I don't."

Spence shrugged. "It's no problem for me."

Natalie gave him directions to her bungalow-style house in Alamo Heights, a few blocks from her parents' home. Spence pulled into the driveway, and Natalie reached for the door handle. His arm shot out to stop her.

"Better let me check it out first," he said. "Where's your key?"

Natalie glanced at him in the dark. "I'm sure everything's fine." Why wouldn't it be? Unless he suspected something. *Knew* something . . .

Natalie couldn't help wondering what Irene's next move might be. And if Spence was in on it.

"Blame it on my training," he said, accepting the key she handed him. He got out of the car, then bent down to ask, "Do you have an alarm?"

She shook her head. The crime rate in her area was low. She'd never felt the need for a home-security system, but as she thought about the phone call she'd received earlier, the threatening tone in the man's voice, she shivered, suddenly glad that Spence was with her.

She watched him disappear inside her house, and then waited for the lights to come on, expecting him to reappear at any moment to give her the all-clear sign. But the house remained dark and he didn't come back.

Minutes passed.

Natalie began to get really nervous. What in the world was keeping him? She hated to think the worst about him, but what if he was in her house, searching through her things, looking for evidence that would convict her of Anthony's murder? He and Anthony had never gotten along, but Spence had said himself tonight at dinner that Anthony had still been his brother, and blood, more often than not, was thicker than water.

And that disconcerting thought brought her back to Irene. Just how far would Spence be willing to go to help his mother? To perhaps get in her good graces for the first time in his life.

Natalie got out of the car and stood for a moment, staring at the darkened house. Something was wrong inside. She didn't know how she knew, but she knew. Something was definitely wrong.

She walked to the front door, pushed it open, and stepped inside. Her hand automatically sought the light switch, and when the light came on, she gasped in terror at the destruction that lay before her.

The room had been thoroughly ransacked. Books had been flung from the shelves, chair and sofa cushions slashed, paintings ripped from the walls. Every vase, jar and glass box had been smashed into a million pieces and every drawer had been jerked free of her desk, the contents dumped on the hardwood floor.

But the cruelest destruction of all was the presents under the Christmas tree. Their colorful paper and ribbons were shredded and crumpled, the boxes plundered.

And Spence was nowhere to be seen.

Natalie stood for a moment, taking in the devastation as her heart hammered inside her. Her fear subsided and anger plunged through her at the violation. These were her things. Her personal belongings. She'd worked long and hard for every last one of them, and now someone had come in here and ruthlessly destroyed her possessions. Her home. Her sanctuary.

Thank God, Kyle wasn't here to see this, she thought. Thank God, he was safe in the hospital with her mother to watch over him. For a split second, Natalie was almost grateful to the driver who had rammed into their car earlier. Otherwise, she and Kyle might both have been at home tonight.

As Natalie gazed around her ruined living room, she realized that whoever had done this would not have let a woman and a small boy stand in his or her way. Whoever had done this had been in a rage, although, for the life of her, Natalie didn't know why.

Then another thought occurred to her. What if whoever had done this was also responsible for the accident earlier? What if it had all been coolly calculated?

Natalie wasn't sure which scenario scared her the most. She started across the floor, her feet crunching on bits of broken glass as she made her way toward the dining room and the kitchen beyond.

She called Spence's name but he didn't answer. A shiver of alarm scurried up her spine. Supposing whoever did this was still here? Supposing Spence had walked in and surprised him? Supposing—

By this time, Natalie's heart and imagination were both working overtime. She tried to calm herself by glancing around, looking for the phone. But a noise from the kitchen startled her again. Someone was in there! She started to turn and run for the front door, but something stopped her; some instinct that told her Spence might be in trouble and need her help.

Without thinking, Natalie crossed the dining room and pushed open the kitchen door. Moonlight poured in through the double windows over the sink, but it still took a moment for her eyes to adjust to the dimness. She reached for the light switch just as her gaze dropped to the figure lying on the floor.

Natalie's heart slammed into her chest. She started forward. A movement just inside the door caught her attention and she whirled, but not in time to save herself. Without warning, something flew out of the darkness to strike her left temple.

White-hot pain pierced through her head, and then mercifully everything went black.

Chapter Nine

Natalie opened her eyes. It took her a moment to get her bearings as she lay there, trying to focus. Trying to remember.

Then it all came back to her. The destruction to her home. The hand flying out of the darkness to strike her. And the body lying on the floor.

Spence!

Natalie tried to get up, but pain shot through her skull and a wave of dizziness washed over her. She tentatively probed her temple with her fingertips, and felt the knot where she had been struck. But when she brought her fingers down, they were dry. No blood, thank God.

Then . . . what were those stains on her clothes? Natalie sat up and stared down at the front of her white blouse. In the moonlight, she could see the dark drips across her chest and for a moment, she wondered if she'd sustained another injury. But other than her head, she felt no pain.

Gingerly she touched the spots on her blouse and found they were still wet. When she lifted her fingertips to her nose, her stomach rolled sickeningly at the unmistakable metallic scent.

Dear God, she thought. It was just like the night Anthony had been murdered. She'd been knocked unconscious, and when she'd awakened, her clothes had been stained with blood. Anthony's blood.

Not again, she thought dizzily. *Please, not again.*

Not Spence.

She struggled to get up, gazing around to find the figure she'd glimpsed on the floor. The moonlight was brilliant enough for her to see blood on her own clothing, but not bright enough for her to locate a body on the floor. There was something wrong with that picture, but Natalie didn't take the time to sort it out. Using the door frame for support, she pulled herself up and felt for the light switch.

Light flooded the room, illuminating every nook and crevice. There was more blood on the floor, along with her glasses, but nothing else. No body. No Spence.

Natalie leaned weakly against the wall, closing her eyes, trying to ignore the pounding in her head. What was happening here? What was happening to her life? How had it suddenly gotten so out of control? She had never felt so helpless, not even when she'd found out she was pregnant. Not even when Anthony had threatened to take away her son if she didn't agree to his terms.

Where, in God's name, was Spence? It seemed he was always disappearing when Natalie needed him the most.

The door beside her opened, and she gasped, jumping back, looking around wildly for something with which to defend herself. But as if summoned by her silent plea, Spence walked through the door.

His presence was hardly comforting. Blood trickled down the side of his face, and his own shirt was splotched with big red circles. His eyes seemed to have a hard time focusing on her.

"Natalie," he said, sounding relieved. "Are you all right?"

"I think so," she said hesitantly. "Are you?"

"At the moment, that's debatable."

He came into the room and Natalie realized for the first time that he was carrying something in each hand—his cell phone in one, and her first-aid kit in the other. He sat down wearily at the kitchen table.

"I've called 911," he said. "The police and an ambulance should be here soon, but maybe you'd better let me have a look at that bump anyway. You were out cold for a couple of minutes."

"What about you?" she asked, bending to retrieve her glasses before coming to sit down beside him. "I saw you on the floor— At least, I thought it was you. Then someone hit me. Next thing I knew, I was waking up and you were nowhere to be found. What happened?"

He grimaced, putting his hand to the cut on his head. "I'm losing my touch, that's what happened. Bastard jumped me from behind. I never even saw it coming."

"Maybe you'd better let me have a look at you," Natalie said. "Judging by all that blood, I'd say you're in worse shape than I am."

"It's nothing," he mumbled, but winced when her fingers explored the cut on his head. "Sorry about your blouse."

"So this *is* your blood." Natalie wondered why that notion didn't particularly relieve her.

"I bent over you to see if you were okay. When I couldn't get you to come around, I decided I'd better get an ambulance over here."

The image of him, hurt and bleeding, disregarding his own wound to tend to her filled Natalie with an emotion she didn't understand. Then again, maybe she did. Maybe that was why her heart was pounding away inside her as she stood over him to tend to his.

"It's not that deep," she told him. "But you may need a few stitches."

"They'll have to wait." He took her arm and pulled her down in the chair beside him. "Before the police get here, there's something you and I need to talk about."

"Like what?"

"Like what happened here tonight."

"But I don't know what happened. I don't know any more than you do."

His green eyes seemed to have no trouble focusing on her now. Cool and relentless, they searched her face. "I think you do know. I think you know a lot more than you've been telling me."

"About what?"

Those same green eyes hardened on her. His every feature seemed to tighten into a mask of cold, dark suspicion. "About Anthony's murder. About the diamonds."

"Diamonds? I don't know—"

"Game's over, Natalie. Where are they? Hand them over before someone else ends up dead."

"What are you talking about? What diamonds?"

Spence watched her, looking for the telltale signs of guilt—dry mouth, darting eyes, trembling fingers.

Natalie displayed none of those as she glared at him. If she was lying, she was a damned good actress.

But hadn't he known that she was? Hadn't he been taken in by her before?

"Where are they?" he repeated.

"I have no idea what you're talking about. I don't know anything about any diamonds."

She looked so bewildered, Spence could almost feel sorry for her, but he wouldn't let himself. He wouldn't let anything dim his assessment of her reaction to what he was telling her. Not even the kiss they'd shared earlier. Not even the memories that kiss had awakened, nor the emotions it had aroused.

He studied her now, wondering if he was doing the right thing by laying his cards on the table. It wasn't in his nature to be so forthcoming, but he needed Natalie's help. And he needed to know if he could trust her.

"The diamonds Anthony was looking for in your store the night he was murdered."

Her eyes widened. "Why on earth was he looking for diamonds in Silver Bells?"

"He came in earlier that day and bought something that he wanted you to deliver, right?"

Her eyes grew even rounder behind her glasses and their blue deepened. "Yes! How did you know that?"

"We had him under surveillance."

"Surveillance? But why?" Suddenly, a light seemed to dawn for her. "Why didn't you tell me this before, when I was trying to convince the police Anthony was looking for something that night? They didn't believe me. Why didn't you come forward and tell them the truth?"

"I had my reasons."

Her eyes flashed with fire, but not the deep, sultry warmth he'd glimpsed earlier when he kissed her. The heat he saw in those blue depths now was pure, unadulterated anger. And in some strange way, it was no less stirring.

"What possible reason could you have to justify withholding information like that from the police? Information that might clear *me.*" Then she said slowly,

"Wait a minute. If you followed Anthony to Silver Bells that day, what about that night, when he was murdered? Were you following him then? Do you know who killed him? *Do you?*"

Behind her wire-rimmed glasses, Natalie's eyes shot daggers at him. Spence thought that he had never seen anyone look so angry, and with good reason, he had to admit. He had withheld things from Natalie and from the police, and now he was going to have to ask her to do the same.

"After Anthony left your shop that day, he went back to his office, where he stayed the rest of the afternoon and evening," Spence told her. "Sometime later, he gave us the slip. We still haven't figured out exactly how he managed to leave the building without our seeing him. But we figure he must have come straight to Silver Bells, somehow got in and turned off the alarm, and was looking for the diamonds when you walked in on him."

She crossed her arms and glared at him. "You still haven't told me why Anthony was looking for diamonds in my shop in the first place."

"We think he meant to send them in the package he had you deliver, only something went wrong. When the package was delivered to the drop, the diamonds were missing."

"But how did you know where the package was being delivered?" she asked incredulously.

"We had an agent in the store while Anthony was there. She got the address off the counter while you were busy with another customer."

"Real cloak-and-dagger-type stuff." Natalie shook her head, unable to believe everything she was hearing.

"More like life-and-death," Spence replied, not wishing to scare her any more than she already was, but knowing he had to impress upon her the seriousness of the situation. "Someone has already been murdered because of those diamonds, Natalie. I don't want to see anybody else get hurt."

She put trembling fingertips to her temple as she gazed at Spence with troubled eyes. The bluest eyes he'd ever looked into, and he had the sudden, almost-irresistible urge to pull her into his arms, to shield her from the dirt that both he and Anthony had wittingly drawn her into.

But now was not the time, and this was certainly not the place. Besides, once he told her the rest of his story, his arms would be the last place she would want to seek shelter, he thought with a stab of bitter remorse.

"Who is it that wants those diamonds?" she asked. "Besides you, I mean."

"Have you ever heard of a man named Jack Russo?"

Something flickered across her features. A glimmer of recognition. Then she shook her head. "Who is he?"

"A crime boss who was arrested three years ago for murdering a diamond dealer in Dallas. The man was killed during a robbery, but the only witness who came forward to testify against Russo was later found dead. There was nothing tying Russo to the murder except the fortune in diamonds that was stolen from the dealer. Anthony was Russo's attorney. He got the murder charges thrown out for insufficient evidence. Russo was later sent to a federal penitentiary on racketeering charges, but he's out now. And the diamonds were never recovered. We think Anthony was holding them for Russo until he got out of prison."

"You mean Anthony deliberately hid evidence from the police that would have sent Russo to prison for murder? Why?"

"Why would he agree to defend a man like Russo in the first place? Anthony isn't here to tell us, but I'm guessing it was greed. Russo probably agreed to give him a cut."

"But Anthony was rich. He was a Bishop."

"Anthony was not rich," Spence said. "At least, not in the sense you mean. He had money—plenty, by most people's standards. But Anthony wasn't most people. He lived an extravagant life-style, and he had an image to uphold."

"What do you mean?" Natalie asked.

Spence got up and walked to the window, staring out into the darkness. "The Bishop family has money, including the law firm and several real-estate holdings worth millions. But my father's will left everything in trust. Everyone gets an allowance—Mother, Anthony, and Anthea—but the bulk of the estate was to be held in trust for the first Bishop grandson."

He turned from the window in time to see the color drain from Natalie's face. She looked beyond shocked. She looked devastated, and Spence's first thought was one of relief. She hadn't known. Anthony hadn't told her about the money.

Her hand fluttered to her heart. "Are you saying—"

"Kyle is the sole Bishop heir."

"Why didn't anyone ever tell me?" she asked in a stunned whisper.

"The terms of my father's will were not something my family wanted to make public. Besides the law firm, the family has always dealt heavily in real estate. If word had gotten out that the Bishop fortune was out of the picture, important deals could have fallen through. Besides the fact that the Bishop reputation had to be maintained. Appearances had to be considered. Mother and Anthony, and even Anthea to a lesser degree, would have been publicly humiliated if it were known they no longer had the Bishop fortune backing them."

"How long have you known about this?" Natalie asked weakly.

"Since before my father died ten years ago. He wanted to make certain I understood certain aspects of the will, so that I wouldn't contest it."

"What aspects?"

"That he had cut me out completely." He said it flatly, with no emotion whatsoever, but Spence could still remember the pain that had knifed through him at his father's arrogant dismissal of him.

"You've refused to do as I say. You've cut yourself off from this family, and now I have no recourse but to do the same to you. You will never get your hands on one cent of Bishop money. Your flagrant disregard for my wishes and this reckless, rebellious behavior you seem to take so much pleasure in flaunting before my face leads me to conclude that any money given to you would not only be ill-spent, but also ill-advised...."

There had been more, but Spence cut off the memories and returned them to where they belonged—in the deepest, darkest recesses of his mind. He focused once again on Natalie and what this information had done to her. Her face was still white and drawn, her whole demeanor so fragile she looked as if she might pass out at any second.

Not exactly the reaction you would expect from someone who had just learned her son would someday inherit a fortune worth millions.

"The trust," she said, still looking dazed. "You said...it was to be held for the first Bishop grandson. Did you mean...Anthony's son?"

"He's the only Bishop grandson."

"I know...but..." She trailed off, as if uncertain how to voice her next question. She took a deep breath, but her eyes refused to meet his. "What if...you had a son first. Would...the money still have gone to Anthony's first son, since you were cut out of the will?"

"That's the strange part." Spence came back over and sat down beside her at the table. "The will stipulated first grandson, not necessarily Anthony's, and I wondered about that, too. But I think I figured out why my father did what he did. He wanted Anthony to marry and have children. At the time of my father's death, Anthony was thirty-one years old, and showed no sign of settling down. That was the only bone of contention between the two of them that I ever knew about. The old man wanted to make sure the Bishop line was carried on, and he knew the one sure way to make Anthony comply with his wishes was to hold the money over his head."

"H-how could he have been so sure Anthony would have the first grandson? What if you had met someone...fallen in love...had children...?" Natalie left the question dangling as she searched his face for some clue, some hint of what he might be feeling. But his face was like a mask, wiped clean of every last emotion.

Was this the same man who had kissed her earlier? The same man who had brought her to her emotional knees with the intense feelings he'd unleashed inside her?

Natalie tried to put the memories of that kiss aside as she concentrated on what he was saying. Because everything he'd told her had hit her with terrific force. Suddenly, so many things became clear, and the past took on a new and more ominous meaning for her. She understood Anthony better than she ever had before. No wonder he'd been so desperate to marry her—and to get custody of Kyle.

"My father knew he could count on Anthony to make sure I stayed out of the picture," Spence was saying. "And I'm equally certain that Anthony was prepared for such a contingency. He knew I'd never cared about the money, so there was no reason for him to think I'd rush out and father a child simply to try and get my hands on the inheritance. But if I'd become serious about someone—fallen in love, as you said..." His words faded away as their gazes held for the briefest of moments. "I'm sure he would have found a willing accomplice and rushed her to the altar in record time."

Like he did me, Natalie thought. Anthony had always taken great pleasure in thwarting his brother at every turn. This must have been the ultimate coup.

"What about Anthea?" Natalie asked.

"My father was a chauvinist of the worst kind. In his eyes, Anthea's children wouldn't have been Bishops. He made that clear in the will, and besides, he knew she would never go against his wishes. Anthea wasn't a threat, but I was, so he pitted Anthony against me in order to force Anthony to carry out his wishes."

And in the meantime, driving Spence and Anthony even further apart, Natalie thought. To make matters worse, she had entered both brothers' lives, and had unwittingly become a part of the drama. And the tragedy...

"I can't believe no one ever told me about this," she said. "Why did your family keep it from me?"

"Probably because they were afraid you would try to get your hands on the money. Everyone else has," Spence said dryly.

"So that's why Anthony was going after custody of Kyle," Natalie said. "He wanted the money."

"Maybe. The trust is protected until Kyle turns twenty-one, but Anthony might have thought it was time he began feathering his nest, so to speak. Getting in Kyle's good graces."

For a moment, neither of them said anything. They didn't have to. Both of them knew what kind of man Anthony had been—greedy, ruthless, and arrogant. And now, it seemed, he'd also been a criminal.

Natalie glanced up, wary. "All of this explains why Anthony would have gotten involved with a man like Russo, and why he would have hidden the diamonds that could have been used for evidence. But what you haven't told me is what happened to those diamonds."

"I was hoping you could tell me."

She'd been in the process of getting up, but that stopped her cold. She looked at him in shock. "You can't still think *I* have them."

"We're almost certain Anthony planted those diamonds in the package he had you deliver. The diamonds were missing when the package arrived a few hours later. We know for a fact the courier went straight from your shop to the delivery address. Unless he somehow managed to unwrap the package, find the diamonds and remove them, then rewrap the box while he was driving, we can pretty much rule him out. That leaves a very small window of opportunity. The diamonds had to have been taken while they were still in your possession."

Their gazes held for the longest moment, and Natalie's heart sank at the suspicion she saw glittering in his eyes. How could he? How could he think she took those diamonds? How could he think her capable of something that devious?

And yet, just a few days ago, hadn't he thought her capable of murder? Put in that context, he probably thought stealing a few diamonds was child's play for her.

Obviously, he'd never known the first thing about her. To think she'd once let him make love to her. To think she'd let him kiss her only a few hours ago. And that, just a few minutes ago, she was wishing he would do it again.

"How could you think that about *me?*" she whispered, feeling the sting of tears threaten behind her lids.

Something flashed in his eyes, a brief emotion that Natalie wanted to believe was regret, but then his gaze hardened in resolve before he glanced away. "I don't know what happened to those diamonds, Natalie, but it's my job to find out. I can't afford to overlook any possibility, dismiss any scenario just because it might be something I don't want to believe. Too much is at stake to let personal feelings get in the way."

"You're right," she said, lifting her chin. She got up and moved away from the table, putting distance between them. "Too much *is* at stake, and I have to look out for myself. So I'm sure you'll understand when I tell you to get out of my house. And don't come back."

"Natalie—" Spence stood, too. The two of them faced each other, and suddenly Natalie's fragile self-control deserted her.

"How dare you?" she cried. "How dare you pretend to help me when all you wanted was to find out where those stupid diamonds are? That's why you bailed me out of jail, isn't it? *Isn't* it?"

"I bailed you out of jail because you didn't belong in there."

"Why?" she demanded. "Because behind bars, I wouldn't be of any use to you? Because I couldn't lead you to the diamonds? Oh, I can't believe I ever trusted you, for even one second." She tore her hands through her hair as she spun away from him. "I should have known better! You're a Bishop. You're all just alike. You don't care who you use. All you care about is getting what you want!" She jerked around to face him again, only to find that his own eyes were blazing back at her.

"Are you finished?"

"No. I've got one more thing to say to you. Get out!"

He grabbed her arms and held her, although Natalie didn't try to run. "I can't do that. The police will be here any minute, and they'll want an explanation for all this. Are you prepared to give them one?"

"I'll simply tell them the truth."

"And look where that got you last time," he reminded her. "Like it or not, you need me. I'm the only one who can help you out of this mess."

"*Help* me? You almost got me *killed*. If you bailed me out of jail so that I could lead you to the diamonds, don't you think Russo thought the same thing? I'm sure that's why I got that threat today."

"What threat?" Spence glared down at her. His hands tightened on her arms.

"Someone called me and said that I had something of his, and he wanted them back. He said he knew where I lived and worked, and where my son was at that moment. He told me to cooperate and no one else had to get hurt."

"Why didn't you tell me about this?"

"Because I had a few other things on my mind," Natalie retorted. "Like your mother threatening to take my son away from me. And then after the accident, after I started thinking about Irene's threat, I didn't think I could trust you...because you were on her side."

"I never said I was on her side," Spence said quietly.

Something in his tone made Natalie's heart start to hammer all over again, but not in fear this time, not in anger.

He'd always had that ability, she thought weakly. Even from the first, when she hadn't known him very well and then later, when she had, he'd always been able to make her want to believe in him.

"You have to trust me, Natalie."

"How can I trust you? You think I'm a thief and a murderer."

"No, I don't."

"But you just said—"

"I said I can't afford to overlook any possibility, regardless of what I might be feeling...for you." His gaze intensified, and Natalie's breath clogged her throat. "You have to trust me. You don't have a choice. You have to let me help you."

"Help yourself, don't you mean?" But her voice had lost some of its resistance. "How can this be happening to me?" she whispered. To her horror, Natalie felt a tear spill over and course down her cheek. She didn't want to cry in front of Spence. She didn't want him to see her weakness; to know that no matter what kind of front she put up, deep down, she was still that same lonely, vulnerable girl he'd once made fall in love with him. And he still had the power to hurt her.

His hands slid up her arms to cradle her face. He thumbed away her tear as he stared deeply into her eyes, and Natalie's heart went wild, despite her mind's objection.

For a moment, time seemed to stop, as they gazed into each other's eyes. Natalie's emotions were at war with her sanity. What sort of hold did this man have over her?

"The police will be here any minute," he whispered, as he rested his forehead against hers.

Dimly, Natalie heard the sirens, still in the distance. But the beating of her heart, the pounding of her blood was so much louder, so much more urgent. She closed her eyes, reveling in the feel of Spence's body so close to hers. Never had she felt so near the edge, and yet, oddly, so protected.

Spence's hand feathered through her hair as his chest lifted in a deep sigh. Natalie thought she knew exactly what he was thinking. What he was feeling. It was strange, in a way. She had once been madly in love with him. He was the first man who'd ever made love to her. And yet now, after all the bitter tears and angry accusations, all the hopeless mistakes and shattered dreams, she had never felt closer to him than she did at this moment.

She drew away and stared up at him, not trusting herself to speak.

"Natalie—" The sirens screamed just outside the house. "Damn." His hands grasped her forearms as he said urgently, "Listen. We have to get our stories straight before they get in here."

"Stories...straight?" Still dazed, Natalie could only look at him in confusion. "What do you mean?"

"The police don't know anything about the diamonds."

"But... we have to tell them. Those diamonds give someone else a motive for Anthony's murder. Like Jack Russo."

He let his hands drop from her arms. "I know, but we can't pin anything on Russo. Without those diamonds, he'll walk again."

"So... you're willing to sacrifice me to catch him?" Natalie couldn't believe what she was hearing. Couldn't believe that just moments ago, she'd been almost ready to start trusting him. "You can't expect me to go along with that."

"Natalie, listen to me." He reached for her again, but she jerked away from him. "In the eyes of the police, this won't change anything. You're still their number-one suspect. Until those diamonds are recovered—"

"Until those diamonds are recovered, you're perfectly willing to have everyone believe I killed Anthony."

"We don't even know for sure Russo killed Anthony."

"But you think he did."

"I think there's an excellent chance of that, yes."

"Then why not tell the police?"

"Because if Russo knows we're on to him, he'll disappear, without the diamonds. And a cold-blooded murderer will go free. Is that what you want, Natalie?"

"And what do *you* want?" she demanded. "Your man, at any cost? What if Kyle and I had been home tonight, Spence? What would have happened to us? Have you thought about that?''

Spence had been thinking of little else ever since he'd walked into Natalie's house and seen the destruction. But when he'd bailed her out of jail, he'd been so sure he could protect her. He hadn't thought Russo would make a move so soon, not until the heat died down over Anthony's murder. But obviously he'd been wrong, and he couldn't afford to make another mistake like that. Not where Natalie and Kyle were concerned.

He wanted to tell her not to worry. That she could trust him; that he would never do anything to harm her or her son. But why should she believe him? Anthony had done a real number on her, and now their mother was threatening to take Kyle away. No wonder Natalie didn't trust any of the Bishops. Spence couldn't blame her, because he didn't trust his family, either.

They stood in the middle of the kitchen floor, eyeing each other warily as car doors slammed outside and the police swarmed into the house.

''Without those diamonds, we don't have anything on Russo,'' Spence whispered. ''If he gets wind of our surveillance, he'll run. But the police will still need someone to pin Anthony's murder on.''

''And that someone is me, isn't it?'' Natalie whispered back, feeling the crushing weight of defeat bearing down on her shoulders.

Spence didn't answer, but his eyes—those Bishop eyes—said it all.

Chapter Ten

The first thing Natalie did when she got back to the hospital was go straight to Kyle's bedside and stare down at him, sending up a prayer of thanks that he was all right.

Her mother was dozing in the chair by the window, and Natalie was careful not to wake her. For once, even her mother's presence couldn't soothe the churning emotions inside her.

First, Spence had kissed her tonight. Then she had gone home to find her house all but destroyed; learned that her son was the sole heir to the Bishop fortune, and that Spencer Bishop had used her once again. Used her to get what he wanted.

He had deliberately put her and her son in danger in an attempt to recover stolen diamonds. For that, Natalie didn't think she could ever forgive him. Especially after she had begun to have a glimmer of hope that she could trust him.

In some ways, Natalie had never felt so betrayed. She hadn't even wanted him to drive her back to the hospital, but after the police had left her house, she'd had little choice, other than call a cab, and she was too anxious to get back to Kyle to wait around for that. So she'd allowed Spence to drive her back here, but the moment he'd walked her to Kyle's room, she'd sent him away.

He'd wanted to come in. Natalie had known that, but by then she'd had enough for one night. Even the argument she'd overheard between him and Sergeant Phillips, who had already been irate for having been called out in the middle of the night, had done nothing to restore her faith in Spence.

If anything, it had only made her feel worse—because he'd been right. The break-in hadn't changed anything. Sergeant Phillips still didn't believe her. He'd looked around at the devastation to her home, then looked at her as if to say, *this doesn't prove anything*.

The phone beside the bed rang, and Natalie reached out to jerk it up before the second ring. Kyle stirred in his sleep, and her mother shifted position in the chair, but neither of them awakened.

It was so late, Natalie couldn't imagine who would be calling. She brought the receiver to her ear and said very softly, "Hello?"

"You got real lucky tonight, lady."

Natalie recognized the gruff voice instantly. It was the same man who had called her at home earlier. The man she now suspected was Jack Russo. Her heart slammed into her chest. "Who is this?"

"I told you before, it doesn't matter who I am. What matters is that you still have what's mine."

"I—I don't know what you're talking about."

"You know exactly what I'm talking about."

Natalie's hand shook so hard she could barely grip the telephone. She remembered what Spence had said earlier, that if Russo knew he was being watched, he would skip town. Somehow she managed to process this information and keep her voice relatively steady as she said, "I don't know who you are or what you want. Why don't you just leave me alone?"

There was a long silence. In a deceptively soft voice, the man said, "How's the boy?"

And then the significance of Russo—if that's who he was—calling Kyle's hospital room hit her. He'd known Kyle was here, just as he'd somehow managed to get her unlisted number. He knew everything about them.

The power of the moment was paralyzing. Natalie had never dealt with anyone like him before. A cold-blooded murderer who had killed once for those diamonds. Who was to say he wouldn't do so again?

"Sorry the kid had to get hurt," the man said, "but I get a little irritated when somebody has something of mine and won't give it back."

"Please," she whispered. "I don't have what you want."

"Then you better find them." The affable note in his voice had vanished, was replaced by an edge as keen as a knife blade. "Because a few scrapes and bruises are nothing compared to what could happen to that kid if you refuse to cooperate. You understand what I'm saying?"

"Yes," she whispered, gripping the phone.

"Good. I'll be in touch and arrange for the drop. I don't think I need to remind you that this little business is just between you and me. The police wouldn't believe you anyway, but they could become a nuisance and then I might really get pissed off."

The line clicked, then went dead. With shaking hands, Natalie hung up the phone. She gazed down at Kyle as her heart hammered in her throat. Dear God, what was she going to do?

She ran the back of her index finger down the side of Kyle's soft cheek. He looked so sweet, lying there. So very defenseless. And her blood froze at the thought of his being in danger. She had to find a way to protect him. Against Russo, against Irene, and maybe even against Spence.

She couldn't let anything else happen to Kyle. Somehow, she had to remove him from harm's way.

No matter what happened to her, she had to find a way to protect her son at any cost.

At *any* cost.

BY THE TIME SPENCE pulled into the circular drive of his family's mansion, the clock on his dash read four minutes past midnight, but he knew his mother would still be up. She always kept late hours, and he didn't want to wait until morning to say what he had to say to her.

If Irene thought that he would back her in a custody suit against Natalie, she'd better think again. He might not be able to do much about the Russo situation just yet, but he sure as hell could alleviate Natalie's fears where his mother was concerned.

The boy belonged with Natalie. That point had been brought home earlier at the hospital, when he'd watched the two of them together. There was no doubt in Spence's mind how much Natalie loved her son, and it gave him cold chills to think about Kyle being taken away from that love and put in this cold, dreary, lifeless house, to be raised by a cold, dreary, lifeless woman who didn't know the first thing about love.

Oh, Irene had adored Anthony. He'd been her idea of the perfect son—handsome, popular, charismatic.

But love? No. Not even Anthony had won Irene's love, because she simply wasn't capable of giving it.

Using the key his mother had given him two days ago when she'd asked him to move back home, Spence let himself in. Almost immediately the butler appeared in the foyer, apparently undaunted by Spence's appearance so late at night.

"Hello, Williams. Is Mother still up?"

"She's retired for the evening, sir."

"How about Anthea?"

"I believe she's still at the office."

"This late?"

"Yes, sir."

"Mind if I wait for her?"

"As you wish. May I get you something to drink?"

"No, thanks. I'll help myself."

Williams nodded curtly, then turned on his heel and disappeared down the hallway. Spence walked into the library and headed for the bar. The night was mild, but the breeze blowing in through the open French doors was distinctly chilly. He crossed the room to close the doors when a sound from outside stopped him.

The French doors opened onto a wide terrace with stone steps that led down to the swimming pool. The pool lights were off, but the moon glimmered in silvery ripples across the surface. The sound came to him again—soft, feminine laughter.

He stepped through the doors onto the terrace. The breeze carried the murmur of voices and the lapping of water against the sides of the pool as he stood there listening to the darkness. Someone was obviously out for a late-night swim.

More whispers, more soft laughter, then silence.

Spence started to go back inside, when a man's voice—low and urgent—said, "When can I see you again?"

He couldn't hear the woman's response, but the man's voice rose angrily. "Don't play games with me! Not after everything I've done for you."

Silence reigned again, during which time Spence assumed the man's anger was somehow being appeased. Then a male figure, tall and muscular, hitched himself from the pool, grabbed a towel from one of the lounges, and took off toward the back of the house.

Spence frowned, not liking the idea of a stranger roaming the grounds. He started to follow the man, but a movement in the pool caught his attention, and for a moment, he watched the slender figure in the moonlight as she cut gracefully through the water. When she turned and came back, Spence was standing at the pool's edge.

Melinda's gaze darted to each side, no doubt wondering if her companion had made a clean getaway. Obviously deciding that he had, she turned back to Spence with a coy smile.

"Well, well," she said. "What brings you calling this time of night?"

"I couldn't sleep."

Her elegant eyebrows rose. "Maybe you're too tense, Spencer. A midnight swim could do wonders for you." She laughed again as she slicked back her red hair with one slim hand. The action lifted her bare breasts out of the water, but she either didn't notice or didn't care. Judging by her demure smile, Spence decided it was probably the latter.

"Come on in," she invited. "The water's great."

"It's the middle of winter, in case you hadn't noticed."

"It's a warm night, in case *you* hadn't noticed, and besides, the pool's heated."

"I'm not in the mood for a swim."

Her voice lowered seductively. "What *are* you in the mood for?"

"I want to talk to you."

Melinda shrugged her shapely shoulders. "Well, if you won't come in, then I guess I'll just have to come out, won't I?"

She stood, and in the moonlight, water ran off her smooth, bare skin like liquid glass. Her long red hair clung to her shoulders in damp clusters, and she slung her head so that the dark tresses hung in ringlets down her back.

Walking deliberately past Spence, she picked up another towel from the lounge and took her time as she blotted herself dry. Then she wrapped the towel around her body and knotted it just above her full breasts as she turned to find Spence watching her.

She smiled knowingly as she picked up a glass from the table beside the lounge and lifted it to her lips. Moonlight sparked off the cut crystal like sunlight on diamonds.

"Who was he?" Spence asked.

"Ah. So you did see." She took a deep drink from the glass. "It was nothing," she said, coming to stand very close to him. "A harmless little dalliance. But I suppose you're going to run straight to Mommy Dearest, aren't you?"

Spence could smell Scotch on her breath. "I don't like the idea of strange men roaming around this house at all hours. You should know better than to bring somebody here."

She reached out and traced a scarlet nail down the front of his jacket. "I didn't bring him here. He lives on the grounds. He's the gardener's son."

"Johnny?"

"He likes to be called John now."

Spence had a vague recollection of a scrawny little boy with a gap-toothed smile helping his father weed the flower beds. A mercenary kid, all too willing to desert his post for more lucrative endeavors, like washing Spence's car. Hardly the image of the muscular man who had climbed out of the pool—and Melinda's arms—a few minutes ago.

"Your grief is touching," Spence said in disgust.

The smile vanished from Melinda's face. She lifted her chin so that he could see the sudden shimmer of tears in her eyes. "I am grieving," she whispered. "But we all have different ways of coping."

"So I heard a few minutes ago."

She at least had the grace to look embarrassed, but only momentarily. Turning, she walked back to the lounge and sat down, crossing her legs in a way that left very little to the imagination. But then, Spence didn't have to imagine. He'd already seen, and the view hadn't moved him. Melinda was a beautiful woman, but she wasn't his type.

She wasn't Natalie.

"No matter what you think about me," Melinda said, her lips quivering in distress, "I loved Anthony. He was my whole world."

"Then you must have been devastated when he told you he wanted a divorce."

Her mouth literally dropped open. A dozen emotions flashed across her face until, after several painful seconds, she seemed to get them all under control. She gave him an outraged glance. "Where in the world did you get an idea like that?"

"Is it true?"

"Of course not! Anthony loved me. We were planning a family together. He wanted children with me. A son by *me.*"

"You were married for six years," Spence observed. "Why wait so long?"

"We saw no hurry. After all, we thought we had years and years ahead of us. How could we have known—" She broke off, and with some effort, squeezed a tear from one eye. With a flourish, she wiped it away with the back of her hand. "How could we have known that woman would destroy everything? She was always so jealous of me. She couldn't stand it that Anthony wanted *me,* that he chose *me* over her. She killed him because she couldn't have him."

With an effort, Spence kept his expression even. "Natalie and Anthony have been divorced for years," he said.

"That didn't matter to her! Anthony told me that she was always coming on to him, begging him to take her back. Her and her...son." She made the last word sound like an unpleasantness that was beyond bearable.

An image of Kyle came to Spence now—the dark, unruly hair, the deep green eyes, and the quick smile that always seemed to have a hint of mischief lurking at the corners.

How could Anthony have ignored Kyle for so long, and then decided, for whatever reason Spence could only guess, that it was time he had custody regardless of how his actions would affect the boy?

Because Anthony had been a ruthless, greedy man. A Bishop. And after tonight, Spence had to wonder if he was really any better. He'd deliberately set out to use Natalie for his own agenda, and regardless of what he'd tried to tell himself over the years, the end did not always justify the means. He'd put her and Kyle's lives in danger, and Spence knew he would have a hard time ever justifying that.

And so would Natalie.

"I don't believe she killed Anthony," he said quietly.

Melinda gasped. "What? Of course, she killed him! Look at the evidence."

"There were no eyewitnesses."

"But she was found kneeling over the body with the murder weapon in her hand. His blood was all over her."

"She was knocked unconscious. When she came to, she tried to see about Anthony, not even realizing the knife had been placed in her hand."

"Oh, please. That's what *she* says."

"I'm inclined to believe her. How else do you explain her workroom being ransacked?"

"She and Anthony struggled. Or, more likely, she did it herself after she killed him, to make herself look like the victim."

"That's what the police seem to think," Spence admitted. "But it all seems just a little too perfect to me. Like someone planned it all out."

"Someone did. *She* did." Melinda's full lips drew together in a practiced pout as she stared up at him.

"What is the matter with you, Spencer? Where's your loyalty to this family?"

That was rich, coming from her. But Spence let it pass, saying instead, "My loyalty belongs with the truth, and I'm beginning to think there might have been someone else who stood to gain more from Anthony's death than Natalie Silver."

Someone who was about to be divorced and cut off without a penny.

Spence didn't say the words, but they hung in the air between them. Melinda's gaze faltered and she turned away, but not before he saw the outrage in her eyes turn to fear. He'd gotten what he came for, Spence thought, turning and walking back toward the house. He didn't need to wait for Anthea after all.

"I CAN'T BELIEVE YOU'RE coming back to work to-day," Blanche said, reaching over to squeeze Natalie's hand. They were having a morning cup of coffee at one of the riverside tables at Delmontico's. "It hasn't been the same without you. Every time I saw that police tape—" She broke off, closing her eyes briefly.

Natalie nodded. "I know. Believe me, I'm not look-ing forward to going back in there, but the police have given their okay, and I can't delay any longer. I've lost too much business, as it is. I've been afraid to even try to calculate the damage." She'd been afraid of so many things lately, especially the threat she'd gotten from Russo last night. He'd said he would be in touch to ar-range the drop, but what would he do when she couldn't produce the diamonds?

Natalie shuddered, thinking about Kyle. He was safe, she told herself, tucked away in her parents' house. Her father had recently installed a state-of-the-art security system, and the neighborhood was regularly patrolled by the police.

He was safe for now, but in the meantime, she'd already begun to make arrangements for her parents and son to leave town. Just in case.

For a moment, Natalie toyed with the idea of confessing all to Blanche. She needed someone to talk to, and for some reason that she couldn't—or didn't want to—understand, she'd done as Spence had asked. She hadn't told the police about Russo and the diamonds, mainly because she didn't think they would believe her—not without Spence backing her up. And he'd made it clear his main objective was nailing Russo.

She sighed deeply, feeling the weight of the world on her shoulders this morning.

"Well," Blanche was saying, "you know I'll help you in any way I can."

Natalie smiled. "You've been a good friend."

Such a good friend that Natalie knew when something was wrong. As wrapped up as she was in her own problems, she could still tell that Blanche wasn't herself. Her complexion looked pale and sickly, and her brown eyes—usually so vibrant—were dull and listless. She looked as if she hadn't slept in days. Even her attire—always a point of pride with Blanche—was drab and unflattering, the baggy, dark green sweater she wore making the shadows beneath her eyes even more pronounced.

"Blanche, is something wrong?" Natalie asked carefully.

"I've been worried sick about you," Blanche said over the rim of her coffee cup.

"I know, but... is there something else? You look so... You don't look yourself."

Blanche smiled ruefully. "I look like hell. Be honest."

"What's wrong?" Natalie asked in concern.

"It's nothing, really. Not compared to your problems." Blanche set down her cup and stared at the dark brew swirling inside.

"It's him, isn't it?"

Blanche looked up, startled. "Him?"

"That man you've being seeing. He's married, isn't he?"

Blanche looked as if she was about to deny it, then she shrugged. "It doesn't matter now, anyway."

"Why? He didn't . . . leave you, did he?"

Blanche's gaze darted away. "You might say that."

"Oh, Blanche. I was afraid something like this would happen. And right before Christmas. I'm so sorry."

"No sorrier than I am."

Natalie leaned toward her and patted the back of Blanche's hand. "He isn't worth it, you know. He isn't worth letting it get to you like this."

Blanche took a deep breath, her eyes on a blackbird that had come to feed on bread crumbs at the river's edge. "I know he wasn't worth it. I've told myself that a hundred times. But it still hurts."

"What are you going to do?" Natalie asked.

"What can I do? Life goes on, doesn't it?" She paused, then said, "What are you going to do?"

"What do you mean?"

"What's the latest word on your case?"

Natalie sat back in her chair and stared glumly at the river. "I talked to my lawyer this morning. The police aren't dropping the charges against me." She'd had some hope that they might after last night, but her attorney had said the D.A. was adamant. A grand jury would have to decide whether or not the evidence against her was sufficient to warrant a trial.

"Meanwhile, like you, I have to get on with my life. And that means reopening the shop."

"How's Kyle taking all this?"

"He's...incredible." Natalie forced a smile and told Blanche about her son threatening to punch Irene Bishop in the nose for thinking his mother was guilty.

For the first time that morning, Blanche laughed. Her mood seemed to lighten a little as they talked about Kyle, but then sobered again when she said, "You don't really think Irene means to take Kyle away from you, do you?"

Natalie shivered in the bright sunlight, thinking about Irene Bishop and her threats, and the revelations Spence had made last night. Just where did Kyle's inheritance fit into Irene's plans?

There was no way Natalie would ever let Irene get her hands on Kyle. Even if it meant making a few revelations of her own. But would that help? Or would it create even more problems? A whole different set of concerns. And threats.

"If she tries," Natalie said, "I'll fight her. There's no way I'll ever let her take Kyle. No matter what I have to do to stop her."

Blanche's eyes looked worried as she gazed at Natalie in distress. "I remember you saying almost exactly the same thing about Anthony. And a few hours later, he turned up dead."

"SHE DIDN'T DO IT."

"The evidence says she did," Sergeant Phillips growled as he shoved a file into his drawer and slammed it shut. "Besides, it's out of my hands. The D.A. thinks there's sufficient evidence to prosecute."

"You could still intervene and you know it," Spence insisted.

Sergeant Phillips shook his head. "That isn't the way it works, and *you* know it. What is it about this broad that has you so worked up, anyway? For an ex-sister-in-law, she certainly seems to have made an impression on you."

Spence ran an annoyed hand through his hair. "Look, I've told you the facts of the case as I know them. I've told you more than I should have."

"Yeah, well, you're a day late and a dollar short as far as I'm concerned. I really don't appreciate the feds waltzing in here and laying claim to one of my cases."

"I'm not doing that. I'm giving you what I know in order to help in your investigation."

Phillips's pale eyes studied him suspiciously. "And what do you want in return? Because if you want the charges dropped against Natalie Silver—"

Spence shook his head. He'd given up on that. "I want you to keep an open mind. I want you to investigate the leads I've given you."

Sergeant Phillips looked down at the paper on his desk. "Interesting list. What about Russo?"

"He's mine."

"Figures." Phillips glanced up. His pale eyes met Spence's and he shook his head. "You are one crazy son of a bitch, you know that? I'd bet my pension that woman's guilty."

"I'm sure you would." Spence rose and planted his hands on the sergeant's desk. "And that's exactly the kind of mind-set that worries me."

BEFORE SPENCE LEFT the area, he went by the local FBI office to pick up a fax he'd received from headquarters. He opened the folder and studied the dossier inside.

The man in the grainy but recognizable photo had gotten out of Joliet Federal Penitentiary six years ago, after having served ten years for manslaughter. Before that, he had been sent up on federal racketeering charges, and before that, for grand larceny. He had been in and out of prison for the better part of his adult life, and had known ties to the mob, in both Dallas and San Antonio.

Spence studied the picture of Frank Delmontico and smiled in satisfaction. He never forgot a face.

"Gotcha," he muttered.

NATALIE UNLOCKED THE front door of Silver Bells and started to step inside, but someone called her name, and she turned to see Frank Delmontico climbing the stairs to the second-story landing.

He was dressed all in black today—black tailored pants and a black silk shirt open at the neck. Two young men—presumably busboys, since they wore stained white aprons over their clothes—followed him up the stairs.

Natalie paused, not understanding why Frank had taken such a sudden interest in her. Since the murder, almost everyone else couldn't distance themselves fast enough from her, but Frank Delmontico chose this particular time to befriend her. Strange, to say the least.

"You're opening your shop today." It was a statement not a question, as if he'd already known she would be here.

Natalie nodded. "The police have given their okay. I guess they've done everything they need to do."

Frank paused for a moment, then said, "Have you been inside since the murder?"

He didn't stumble or look away when he said "murder." In a way, his bluntness was something of a relief. Natalie shook her head. "No. This is the first time."

"Then no one's been in to clean up."

At first Natalie thought he was talking about the broken glass and debris in her office, but then she realized he meant the blood. Her stomach took a sickening jolt at the crimson memory of that night.

"That isn't something a woman should have to do," Frank said.

Natalie's mind was only half on what he was saying. "What isn't?"

"The cleanup. My boys will do it for you." With a jerk of his wrist, he summoned the two young men and they stepped forward, eager to take charge.

Natalie was touched, but at the same time, she didn't quite know what to think. "Why... why would you do this for me? You don't even really know me."

Frank shrugged. "It isn't something a woman should have to do," he repeated, as if that were explanation enough. "My boys are trustworthy. You don't have to worry about that."

"I'm not." But Natalie realized that on the fringes of her mind, she had been. Perhaps everything she'd been through had jaded her, made her too ready to distrust someone's motives. She didn't like that about herself. It was too... Bishop-like.

She forced herself to smile gratefully. "Okay. I accept your offer. Thank you."

Frank smiled, too. "Don't you worry. My boys will take care of everything."

AND THEY DID. Two hours later Natalie stood in her office and gazed around. The glass and debris had been swept away, the books and packaging returned to the shelves, and the contents of her desk drawers neatly stacked on her desk. The only thing to remind her of that awful night was the dark water stain on the carpet where they had scrubbed away the blood.

As she stared at the stain, the horror of that night came rushing back to her. She'd tried to forget, but there was no way she ever would. The moment she'd opened her eyes and turned her head to see Anthony lying on the floor beside her, his blood covering them both...

She put her hands to her eyes, trying to block the images. Her cheeks were wet with tears, and she rubbed her fingertips across them.

"So it's true," someone said behind her. "The murderer always returns to the scene of the crime."

Natalie spun at that voice. Anthea stood in the doorway, clad in a dark pin-striped suit with a double-breasted jacket and man-tailored slacks. She wore loafers, carried a briefcase, and her short, dark hair was heavily gelled and combed straight back from her unmade-up face.

Caught off guard, Natalie stared at her for a moment, realizing she'd forgotten how tall Anthea was. Almost as tall as Anthony had been. In fact, she looked very much like her twin brother today. The resemblance was...startling.

Seemingly unaware of the effect her appearance had on Natalie, Anthea walked into the office, then stopped short, her gaze dropping to the water stain on the floor. As if in fascination, she studied it for a long moment before lifting her green eyes to meet Natalie's. "Do you really think a little water will wash away what you've done?"

"What do you want, Anthea?" Natalie asked wearily, in no mood to proclaim her innocence yet again.

Anthea's gaze darted to the floor, then lifted. "I'm here to offer you a deal."

Natalie was immediately suspicious. "What kind of deal?"

Anthea plopped her briefcase on the desk and snapped open the locks. She lifted the lid to reveal neat stacks of twenty-dollar bills.

"Two hundred and fifty thousand dollars. A quarter of a million. How long would it take you to make that kind of money here?"

Considering what the publicity surrounding Anthony's murder and her arrest would do to her business, Natalie didn't even want to speculate.

"It's yours," Anthea said. "All you have to do is strike a bargain with me."

Natalie had a feeling that would be like bargaining with the devil, and that the ultimate price might very well be her soul. "I don't make bargains," she said, remembering the one she had struck with Anthony and what it had cost her.

"I think you might want to change your mind." Anthea's gaze was as hard as concrete. "I want you to take this money and get out of town. Leave the country. Take your son and don't either one of you ever come back."

"Why?" Natalie demanded. "If you think I'm guilty, why help me leave town?"

Anthea shrugged. "Because it would be easier that way. You would be out of our lives for good, and Mother wouldn't have to go through the torment of a trial, hearing the gruesome details of Anthony's death, facing reporters and their endless questions day in and day out. I don't want her to go through that."

"If I run, I'll look guilty," Natalie said.

"And if you don't, I'll make your life a living hell. I'll personally see to it that you're put away for life. And Mother will get Kyle. Anthony's precious son."

Something in her tone sent a cold chill up Natalie's spine. The way she looked when she talked about Kyle. The flash of hate that filled her eyes. The barest hint of rage that colored her voice.

For a moment, Natalie stared at the money. A quarter of a million dollars would solve a lot of her problems. She and Kyle could simply disappear, get away from the danger that faced them here. They could go someplace where Russo—and the Bishops—would never be able to find them.

But running never solved anything, and Natalie knew that by taking Anthea's money, she would only be making her situation worse. She would never be free of the Bishops, no matter how far and how fast she ran. Because every time she looked into her son's eyes, they would be there, mocking her from those green depths.

Her hands were shaking as she reached over and slammed the briefcase shut. "Take your filthy money and get out of here, Anthea. And don't *ever* let me catch you near my son. Do you understand me?"

One thick eyebrow rose in mock disdain. "Oh, I understand you, Natalie. Better than you think." She snapped closed the locks on the briefcase. "You're making a big mistake. This is the only Bishop money you or your son will ever get your hands on.''

''I don't want your money. Any of it. I just want your family to leave Kyle and me alone.''

The eyebrow arched again. ''Does that include Spencer?'' When Natalie refused to answer, Anthea smiled coolly. ''I thought not.''

She jerked up the briefcase and turned toward the door, very deliberately striding across the dark stain in the middle of the floor.

Chapter Eleven

Christmas music played softly from overhead speakers, and the tiny white lights on the Christmas tree glowed in the gloom of late afternoon. Natalie busied herself checking stock. There was a lot to do, and she tried to tell herself it was a good thing she'd had so few customers that afternoon.

But who was she trying to kid? The holiday season was a complete disaster, and with only a few more days until Christmas, there wasn't much hope of salvaging it. The shop should have been a hub of frenzied activity, but only two people—an elderly couple shopping for their granddaughter—had stopped in.

It was just after six and the three hours until closing loomed before Natalie like miles and miles of bad road. In the deep silence of the store, with only the recorded Christmas carols to buoy her spirits, she found it difficult not to dwell on her problems. Suddenly, it all seemed too much. Natalie dropped her head in her hands, not wanting to give in to the despair, but somehow no longer feeling able to fight it.

When the bells over the door pealed, she hastily wiped her face with the back of her hand, and plastered on a smile as she walked around the counter to greet her customer. The smile slid from her face as she saw who stood inside her doorway.

"This must be my lucky day," she said, hoping the telltale traces of tears had been wiped clean from her face. She lifted her chin and glared at Spence. "First Anthea, and now you."

But in spite of her bravado, she couldn't help the tiny thrill of nerves that coursed down her spine at the sight of him. He wore jeans, faded and snug, and a dark collarless shirt that did interesting things to his eyes. His face was shadowed with just the barest hint of beard, making him look a little too dangerous in the deserted confines of her shop.

He looked at her in surprise. "Anthea was here? What did she want?"

"She offered me a bribe to leave town. A quarter of a million dollars."

"Damn," Spence muttered. "What the hell is she up to?"

"I don't know and I don't care," Natalie said. "I just want her—and the rest of your family—to leave me alone. And that includes you."

Something flashed in his eyes. Something dark and...deadly. "I can't do that, Natalie. Like it or not, we're in this together and we need to talk." Slowly he walked toward her.

She had to fight the urge to retreat, not because she thought he would physically harm her, but because she didn't quite trust herself in his presence. The memory of his kiss—and what it had done to her—was still too fresh.

"About what?" She forced her tone to remain wary. "Didn't you say enough last night? I did what you asked me. I didn't tell the police about Russo, and now, because of that, I may have to send my son into hiding."

"What do you mean?"

"I mean Russo is still threatening me. He called me at the hospital last night after you dropped me off. At least, I'm assuming it was Russo. Naturally, he didn't identify himself. He implied the car accident yesterday was a warning, and that if I didn't cooperate, something worse would happen. He said he would be in touch to arrange the drop, and that if I went to the police—" She broke off, shuddering at the memory of Russo's threat.

"What else did he say?" Spence asked, his voice hard.

"Nothing. But what happens when he calls to arrange the drop?" Natalie asked desperately. "What happens when I can't produce the diamonds? Because no matter what you or anyone else thinks, I don't have them."

Spence came to stand directly in front of her, staring down at her. "I know you don't. But I had to make sure."

"If that's supposed to make me feel better, it doesn't." She turned away, fiddling with a price tag on a blue and silver wreath as she tried to pretend his nearness had no effect on her. There could be any number of reasons for her shortness of breath, the hammering of her heart.

"I'm sorry you had to get dragged into all this."

Natalie could feel his warm breath on the back of her neck, and she was afraid to move an inch, afraid to turn her head and discover just how close he was.

"I never meant for you and Kyle to be put in any danger."

She did turn then, slowly, her gaze lifting to his. "Kyle is my whole world. If anything happens to him, I will never forgive you."

The bleakness in her eyes took Spence's breath away. She stood only to his shoulder. She seemed so small and fragile at that moment—so very vulnerable. And yet he sensed an inner strength, a steely determination to protect her son at any cost.

His mother didn't know it yet, but she was up against a formidable opponent, he thought, not without some pride.

Natalie's straight brown hair fell softly against the sides of her face, and with an effort, he restrained himself from reaching out to tuck a loose strand behind her ear. She wore a short gray skirt that showed off her slender legs, and a dark blue sweater that deepened the blue of her eyes behind her glasses. In spite of the obvious weariness in her face, Spence thought that she had never looked more beautiful. More desirable.

Memories of the kiss they had shared last night flashed through him, and he found himself wanting to kiss her again. And again.

With an effort, he shook off those forbidden urges. Now was not the time, and besides, he had the distinct impression Natalie just might slap his face if he tried to kiss her today. After last night, he could hardly blame her.

"I want to talk about that window of opportunity we discussed last night. If we can find those diamonds, all our problems will be solved." He deliberately moved away from her. He wanted to think the flicker of emotion in her eyes was disappointment, but he knew better. He'd seen Natalie's anger too many times in the past few days to mistake it for anything else.

"Who else had access to that package before the courier picked it up that day?" he asked.

"No one. I boxed it up myself."

"Are you sure? Think hard. A lot's happened since then. Something may have slipped your mind."

Natalie sighed, wanting to object to his demands on principle, but knowing her cooperation was too important. Her life depended on it, and so might Kyle's.

She began to pace back and forth as she thought out loud. "Anthony came in around four o'clock. He was supposed to take Kyle to a Spurs game that night, so I thought that was why he was here, even though Kyle wasn't home from school yet. He was late because he was in a race after school that day. Anyway, Anthony said he wanted to do some shopping for the mother of one of his clients. He said . . . his client had been away for a long time."

"Yeah, in Joliet," Spence said dryly.

"He looked around for a long time. Finally, he asked to see a music box. It was an Étienne—" she started to explain, then waved her hand impatiently. "It had a secret compartment that seemed to particularly appeal to him."

"I'll bet. Go on."

Natalie shrugged. "That's it. He bought the music box."

"Did you ring it up for him immediately?"

Natalie frowned in concentration. "No. Some customers came in and he told me to wait on them first. I thought it was an unusual request for Anthony, but he insisted he wasn't in any hurry. But after the customers left, he acted as if he couldn't wait to get out of here. He didn't even wait for Kyle."

"Can you remember anything special about any of the customers? Did anyone act suspicious, overly nervous, anything like that?"

Natalie shook her head. "I remember it was extremely busy that day." She glanced around her empty shop, thinking ironically how she had lamented being shorthanded that day. If only that was her problem now. "I don't remember anything special about any of them. Nobody caught my attention, not even the FBI agent you sent in," she added with an edge of sarcasm.

Spence refused to rise to the bait. "What did you do with the music box after Anthony left?"

"I took it back to my workroom and put it on my desk. I remember getting down packaging material and a label, and then I called the delivery service to pick it up."

"Did you leave the box in your workroom?"

"I'm pretty sure I did. Kyle came in then, and after that, things got even more hectic. When Michelle—she's the high-school student who works...worked for me part-time during the Christmas season—came in, I asked her to make out the shipping label and get the package ready for the courier."

"So you didn't actually see the music box again?"

Natalie shook her head. "I guess I didn't."

"And then the courier picked it up just before six," Spence said.

"You said last night he didn't have enough time to open the package, find the diamonds, then repack the box before he delivered it. So that just leaves me, doesn't it?" Natalie asked, the despair overcoming her again.

"And this Michelle, you mentioned."

"But she's just a kid," Natalie protested. "I've known her and her parents for ages."

"I still want to talk to her."

Dear God, Natalie thought. When would it end? How many more innocent people had to be dragged into this dirty business before it was resolved? Who else would have to get hurt?

She put her hands to her face. "This is a nightmare," she whispered.

Gently, Spence removed her hands. He held them in his own hands as he gazed down at her. "Just hang on a little while longer," he said. "We'll get to the bottom of all this. I promise you that."

"If it was just me," Natalie said, "I could take it. But Kyle... I can't stand to think of him being in danger. What am I going to do?"

Spence's hands slid up her arms, and before Natalie quite knew how it happened, she was in his embrace. He held her close, and for the first time in a long time, Natalie felt completely safe. She knew it was only an illusion, but that didn't seem to matter at the moment. She laid her head against his shoulder and sighed.

"I won't let anything happen to you or Kyle." His voice was a low rumble in his chest. She could feel his heart beating beneath her hand, and its steady cadence gave her a measure of comfort.

Natalie closed her eyes, wanting to believe him. "You may not be able to stop it. Spence..." Her voice trailed off in a quiver. "I'm so afraid for Kyle. He's staying with my parents because I thought he would be safer away from me. But if Russo found us at the hospital—"

"Kyle's safe, Natalie."

"How can you be so sure?"

"The house is being watched."

She drew back and gazed up at him. "By whom?"

"Some friends of mine."

"Agents?"

Spence nodded. "You can trust them. They're the best in the business. There's no way anyone can get to Kyle."

"But... how did you know he was with my parents?"

"I called the hospital early this morning. Your mother told me you were taking him to their house."

"She wasn't supposed to tell anyone," Natalie said worriedly.

"Maybe she thinks I'm not just anyone."

Their eyes met, and Natalie sensed that something important was happening between them. Something inevitable.

He *wasn't* just anyone, and they both knew it.

She drew a deep, shuddering breath as their gazes held. "Thank you for protecting my son," she whispered.

He touched his fingertips to her face—a butterfly caress that Natalie felt all the way to her soul.

SINCE BUSINESS WAS SLOW—nonexistent, in fact—Natalie closed shop early, and she and Spence drove to her house to have another look around.

"What exactly are we looking for?" she asked, as she let them in and flipped the light switch. Although she knew what to expect, the way her living room had been torn apart still shocked her. She gazed around, trying to suppress her tears.

"I'm not sure," Spence admitted. "I just want to have another look. Something doesn't fit—"

"Like what?"

As if he were a diviner looking for water, Spence slowly walked around the room. "What is it?" he muttered. "What am I missing?"

Watching him, Natalie was struck by the realization of just how far they'd come since he'd walked into that interrogation room a few days ago. Until then, she hadn't seen him in seven years, and she had been filled with distrust, anger, and not a small amount of fear.

Now they were working together to protect her son and clear her of a murder charge. Natalie wasn't sure when she had decided to trust him. She'd had no one else to turn to and he had volunteered for the job. But it was more than that, and she knew it.

What she was feeling for Spencer Bishop was more than gratitude, and she would be a fool not to acknowledge it, to pretend it wasn't there, or that it would somehow go away.

Because it wouldn't. Not in seven years had her feelings for him disappeared. Oh, there was still a residual anger inside her for what he had done to her. For having misled her. For having made love to her when he had been engaged to another woman. For having left her desperate enough to believe in Anthony.

But there were other emotions that remained. The attraction, of course, but that was the least of it. When she thought about the way he had been raised, how he had been shunned by his family—his own mother— Natalie wanted to reach out and draw him into her world. When she glimpsed the bleakness in his eyes, the loneliness in his soul, she wanted to wrap her arms around him and show him what it meant to be loved.

That thought startled her. That she was even contemplating giving her love to Spencer Bishop again was a frightening prospect. He'd hurt her terribly once, and because of that pain, she'd done something that had changed her life forever. Spence's, too, although he didn't know it. What if he found out? What if he somehow learned that—

"Kyle?"

"What? I—I'm sorry," she stammered. "I wasn't listening."

Spence looked at her strangely. "You said Kyle came into the shop that afternoon. Was anyone with him?"

"Oh, that. Blanche picked him up after school and brought him to the shop. Then a little while later, Wendy, his baby-sitter, came by and got him."

"Did any of them have access to the package?"

Natalie frowned. "No. Blanche stayed and talked for a while, but she never went back to the workroom. Neither did Wendy."

"What about Kyle?"

Natalie glanced at him in surprise. "What about him?"

"Was he in the workroom at any time?"

In spite of her previous thoughts, Natalie's hackles rose. "He's just a little boy! You're not suggesting—" Her hand flew to her mouth. She looked up at Spence. "My God," she whispered. "He went back to the workroom to get a present I'd boxed for his teacher."

"In the same kind of box Anthony's music box was in?"

She nodded.

"Same size?"

She swallowed and nodded again.

"What happened to the box he brought home?"

"I assumed he put it under the tree." They both turned and stared at the ravaged presents under her tree.

In unison, they crossed the floor and began to scavenge through the opened boxes and ripped paper.

After a few moments, Natalie sat back. "It isn't here."

"What do you think he could have done with it?"

"I have no idea."

"You said it was a present for his teacher. Is there a possibility he already gave it to her?"

Natalie shook her head. "He hasn't been back to school since that day. And besides, he wouldn't have taken it until the Christmas party, which is tomorrow."

"Then there's only one thing to do," Spence said.

They both turned and headed for the front door.

KYLE SAT ON THE SOFA, one knee drawn up as he picked at a scab on the top of his foot. It was late, and Natalie had awakened him from a deep sleep. He wore Wolverine pajamas, his dark hair was tousled—cowlicks sticking out in all directions—and the look on his face was anything but that of a happy camper.

"What'd I do?" he asked, his gaze bouncing back and forth from Natalie to Spence.

"Maybe nothing," Natalie said, trying to ignore the wide, innocent eyes he turned on her. "We just need to ask you a few questions."

"Have you ever heard of the FBI?" Spence asked, taking out his badge and showing it to Kyle.

Kyle's green eyes widened. "Am I under arrest?"

Natalie saw Spence smother a quick grin as he sat down in the chair across from them. "No, you're not under arrest. I need your help with one of my investigations."

Kyle sat up straighter, suddenly looking wide-awake. "No kidding? Really?" When Spence nodded, Kyle asked, "Do I get a gun?"

"Absolutely not," Natalie said.

Kyle turned back to Spence. "Do you have a gun? Can I see it?"

"Maybe later," Spence replied, flashing Natalie an apologetic glance. "What I want to do now is ask you a few questions."

"Oh." Kyle looked thoroughly disappointed. "But I don't think I should talk to you."

Again, Natalie caught the surprise in Spence's eyes. Obviously he hadn't been around six-year-old boys very much if he thought interrogating one would be easy. Kyle was always one step ahead of her, and she suspected he would be no different with Spence, FBI agent or not.

"Why not?" Spence asked.

"I heard my dad tell someone on the phone that you should never talk to the cops unless you have your attorney with you."

"I hear you," Spence said. "But your mother can represent you. You trust her, don't you?"

Kyle rubbed his nose and considered. "Okay."

For the next several minutes, Spence questioned Kyle gently about the day Anthony was killed. When he came to the subject of the teacher's present, Kyle suddenly became fascinated once again with the scab on his foot.

"Kyle," Natalie said. "What did you do with Miss Riley's present? It's not under the tree."

"I hid it," Kyle said. "Because I didn't want robbers stealing it."

The irony of his words was not something Natalie could appreciate at the moment.

"Where did you hide it?" she asked.

"I forget."

Natalie held her breath, waiting for Spence's temper to erupt or, at the very least, for his patience to wear thin, but he merely said softly, "Think real hard, Kyle. This is important. Remember, I need your help."

Kyle seemed to take this under advisement. He scratched his head, then turned to stare up at Natalie. "What do you think I should do, Mom?"

"If you know where the present is, I think you should tell him, Kyle. He's right. This is very important."

"Will it help you?"

"It might."

He nodded, then turned back to Spence without hesitation. "It's in my tree house."

Spence and Natalie exchanged glances. Spence stood and offered Kyle his hand. "You've been a big help," he said solemnly. "If I crack this case, I'll put your name in for a citation."

"Okay," Kyle said, shaking Spence's hand. "But I'd rather have a Super Nintendo."

Chapter Twelve

In the moonlight, the diamonds winked at them. Perched in Kyle's tree house, Natalie stared in fascination at the flash and sparkle of the gemstones. The half dozen or so—a mere sampling of what they had found in the music box—nestled in Spence's palm were each several karats in weight and more brilliant than wildfire at midnight.

Natalie caught her breath. To think that lives had been lost because of those diamonds. To think that she and Kyle were still in mortal peril because of those bits of cold stone glittering against Spence's palm.

They had found the music box, along with an odd assortment of action figures, broken pencils and crayons, and a few items Natalie had yet to identify, inside the old metal army locker her father had given to Kyle. The two of them had hauled it up to Kyle's tree house one afternoon, and Kyle called it his treasure chest—an apt description, considering.

Using the flashlight they'd brought along, Natalie rummaged inside the locker, wondering what else Kyle might have squirreled away up here and forgotten about. She examined and discarded several items, then, toward the bottom, saw something that looked familiar to her.

"What is it?" Spence asked, still cradling the diamonds in his fist.

"It's an antique ivory comb," Natalie said, holding it out to him.

Spence took the comb and studied it briefly before handing it back. "Looks expensive."

"It is. It belongs to Blanche. I can't imagine how Kyle got it."

Spence glanced up. "You don't think he stole it, do you?"

Natalie winced at his bluntness. "No. He wouldn't do that. He may hide things and forget where he puts them, but he would never intentionally take something that didn't belong to him." Natalie frowned as she slipped the comb into her pocket. Blanche must be worried sick about it. The comb had belonged to her grandmother, and was one of Blanche's most prized possessions.

Tomorrow, Natalie would have to find out how her son got that comb, and then she would make sure it was returned to Blanche, safe and sound. But for now, there was still the matter of the diamonds and Jack Russo to worry about.

Spence opened the velvet pouch, and Natalie caught the flash of fire as he let the stones slide back inside.

She looked up and met his gaze. "What do we do now?"

"We have our bait," he said, stuffing the diamonds into his jacket pocket. "Now we set our trap."

"WHAT HAPPENS IF RUSSO doesn't call?"

"He'll call," Spence said. "Those diamonds can buy him a new life."

"But what if he finds out who you are? What if he thinks I've gone to the FBI? He specifically warned me not to go to the police," Natalie reminded him.

"Even if Anthony told him I'm with the Bureau, there's still no reason for Russo to be overly suspicious of my presence. As Anthony's brother, I have a legitimate reason for being in San Antonio. And for being around you," he added, gazing down at her.

Natalie shivered. They were standing on the balcony of Spence's hotel room overlooking the Riverwalk. After finding the diamonds, they'd both agreed that it wasn't a good idea for her to go back to her parents' house. She was the one Russo was after, and the farther she stayed away from Kyle, the better.

But gazing up at Spence now, seeing the reflection of moonlight in his eyes, she wasn't so sure this was such a good idea, either. The danger and drama of the last few days had drawn them closer together, rekindled an old flame Natalie had hoped was long dead.

She'd tried to deny it—to herself and to Spence—but now she couldn't, and for the first time in a long time, she allowed herself to wish for the impossible. She wished they could go back seven years and start all over.

For a while, neither of them said anything. A breeze gusted across the balcony and Natalie wrapped her arms around herself as she stared down at the Christmas lights reflected on the river.

A thousand regrets washed over her. She'd made so many mistakes. Trusted the wrong people. And now she'd come full circle. Spencer Bishop was back in her life, and she was feeling things she had no business feeling; wishing for things that could never be.

Finally, unable to bear the silence any longer, she asked, "Why did you never marry, Spence?"

She wasn't looking at him, but she sensed his surprise at the question. Sensed his shrug. "In my line of work, it's easier not to be tied down."

He said it so flatly, with no trace of emotion, that the line sounded practiced, as if he'd been telling himself that same thing for a long, long time. She gave him a sidelong glance. "Is that why you didn't marry... her? Because of your job?"

He frowned in the moonlight. "Her? I don't know who you're talking about."

Natalie turned to face him. "I'm talking about *her*. The woman you were engaged to while you were... seeing me," she said, more bitterly than she'd intended.

Spence looked genuinely perplexed. "I repeat, I don't know who or what you're talking about, Natalie. Why do you think I was engaged?"

"I... was told you were."

"By whom?"

"Anthony."

She saw him stiffen. Saw his eyes darken with anger and something else she couldn't quite define. "Then he lied to you. I wasn't seeing anyone but you. There was never anyone else."

Natalie's breath backed up in her throat. She didn't dare believe what he was telling her could be true. "But he showed me pictures—"

"You mentioned something about pictures that day at his funeral," Spence interrupted. "What kind of pictures?"

Natalie's hand was shaking as she lifted it to push back her windblown hair. "Pictures of you... and a woman. A beautiful woman. Anthony said she was your fiancée."

A muscle in Spence's jaw tightened. "When did all this happen?" His voice was edged with an emotion that almost frightened Natalie, and his eyes deepened with an intensity that took her breath away.

"It was a few weeks after you'd left," she said. "He came to me at work one day and said he needed to talk to me. He took me to lunch and told me very gently that you weren't the man I thought you were. When he saw how upset I was, he got angry at you and he said I shouldn't blame myself, because you had a history of using women—pretending to care about them until you got what you wanted—and then just leaving them. He said the reason you left San Antonio so abruptly wasn't because you had an assignment back in Washington, but because you had a fiancée. He showed me pictures of you and her together and then he said...he said she was the reason why I couldn't call you. And why you never called me."

"I did call you," Spence said. "At work one day. Anthony answered the phone. I gave him a number to give to you. He said he would."

"He didn't."

"I wondered why you didn't call," Spence said. "So I called you another time, at your apartment. Anthony answered again."

"It must have been one of the days he took me home from work. I was sick...." Natalie trailed off, not wanting to explain further, then asked, "What did he tell you?"

Spence's voice was like ice. "He said he'd given you the number and you'd thrown it away. He said you didn't want to talk to me, because the two of you...the two of you were together."

Natalie gasped. "No! We weren't. Not then...not until..."

"Until when?" If possible, his eyes grew even icier.

Natalie said in a rush, "He never gave me your phone number. I didn't know how to get in touch with you, and the longer you were gone, the more everything he said made sense. I started to believe that you had lied to me, that you had used me, and I felt so humiliated. So ashamed."

Spence's hands balled into fists at his sides. He said very quietly, "If Anthony wasn't already dead, I believe I could kill him. My own brother."

Natalie's heart started pounding painfully inside her. Anthony was the one who had lied to her. He was the one who had used her. Not Spence.

She should have known. Somehow she should have known, but even after she'd learned what kind of man Anthony really was, even when she'd questioned whether what he'd told her about Spence was true, she'd done nothing about it, because by that time, she hadn't trusted any of the Bishops. She'd been hurt too deeply, and by that time, there had been too much at stake to allow her feelings to cloud her judgment.

Dear God, she thought. *How could I have been so wrong?*

She closed her eyes against the wave of emotion rolling over her. "Why?" she whispered. "Why did he go to all that trouble to keep us apart?"

"For the money," Spence said flatly. "He saw that you and I were getting close, that what we had...was something special, and he was probably worried that when I came back, we might eventually marry. He must have thought that he not only had to get a wife of his own, but that he had to somehow keep you and me apart." He had been pacing the balcony, but now he spun to face her. His green eyes flashed with unexpected fire. "And you made it easy for him, didn't you? What did you think, Natalie? That if you couldn't have one brother, you'd take the other? The richer, more powerful Bishop?"

His words stung her to the quick. "No! It wasn't like that. I thought I'd lost you. I thought you'd lied to me, used me—"

"And so you fell into Anthony's arms the moment my back was turned."

"It wasn't like that," Natalie repeated, trying to calm her racing heart, trying to stem the rising tide of her own anger. "I married Anthony for all the wrong reasons. I admit that. I was hurt and ashamed and... on the rebound from you. But from the very first, I knew what a horrible mistake I'd made. I paid dearly for what I did." Her eyes flooded with tears and she turned away quickly, before Spence could see how deeply his words had wounded her.

There was a long silence, then Spence asked, "If the marriage was such a mistake, why didn't you leave him? Why didn't you get an annulment?"

"I tried to, but you don't just walk out on a Bishop," Natalie said bitterly. "There were ... complications."

"Kyle?"

She nodded, still not daring to look at him. "He threatened to take the baby away from me if I didn't agree to stay with him, at least until after Kyle was born. He said he would prove in court I was an unfit mother. He said evidence could be created and judges could be bought, and I believed him. I knew he could do it, because by that time, I'd found out what kind of man he really was. I'd seen just what he was capable of." Impatiently, she wiped the back of her hand across her wet cheek.

"If you knew what kind of man he was, you never thought to doubt what he'd told you about me?" The question compelled her to face him. His eyes burned into hers, and Natalie wanted to look away again. To run away before his accusations turned into something darker.

But she couldn't, because she knew if she left now, there would be no coming back. No second chances. And even though something told her that might be for the best, she couldn't bring herself to leave him. Not like this. Not with the ugliness Anthony had created still wedged between them.

She took a deep breath. "I might have doubted what he told me . . . if it hadn't been for Anthea."

"What did she have to do with it?"

"She told me virtually the same thing Anthony had. That you were about to be married, and that your . . . fling with me wasn't your first and probably wouldn't be your last."

"So he got her to lie for him," Spence said, his voice more resigned now than angry. He turned and rested his forearms against the balcony railing, gazing down at the water. "Anthea always did whatever Anthony asked of her. Her devotion to him—and her contempt for me—was the only thing that ever endeared her to our mother, and Anthea knew it. She knew how to play the game. I never learned."

"I'm sorry," Natalie said, not knowing what else to say. She ached to touch him, to comfort him, but he seemed so remote. So . . . cold.

"It doesn't matter anymore."

But Natalie sensed that it did still matter to him. A great deal. Not for the first time, she tried to imagine what it had been like for him, growing up in that cold, dismal household, knowing there was no one he could turn to, no one who cared about him. He had never been taught how to love, and Natalie thought that was the saddest legacy of all.

She stared at his silent profile, wondering what he would do if she wrapped her arms around him and laid her head against his shoulder. Would he push her away? Somehow she didn't think he would, but it was a chance she wasn't yet willing to take.

After a few moments, he started talking again, but he didn't look at her. Instead he continued to stare out into the darkness. "When I came back and found out that you had married Anthony, I could have strangled you both with my bare hands." She saw his knuckles whiten on the railing. "But even then, as angry as I was, I was still so crazy about you I wanted to come to you and ask you to leave him, to give us a second chance."

Natalie's heart skipped a beat. Her breath tightened in her throat. "Why didn't you?" she whispered. Her hand touched his sleeve before she could stop herself, and he turned suddenly to stare down at her.

"Because Anthony got to me first. He told me you were the one who came on to him, the moment I'd left town. He said the marriage was your idea."

Natalie shook her head. "It wasn't. I swear—"

"I know that now," Spence said grimly. "But back then, even knowing what Anthony was capable of, I thought the proof was pretty damning. You were married to him, after all, and I'd only been gone a short while."

Although nothing should have surprised her by now, Natalie stood speechless, reeling from his words as if each one of them had been a physical blow. "That's why you looked at me with such contempt that day. Such hatred. I might have come to you, too, told you...everything, if it hadn't been for that look in your eyes. I've never forgotten it."

Without Anthony's lies coloring her perception, Natalie suddenly had a clear vision of what Spence's homecoming must have been like for him. For the first time in his life, he thought he had someone waiting for him who loved him—and then to find out that she had married his brother behind his back...

"I'm so sorry," she whispered. "I'm sorry for everything you had to go through."

He stared down at her, his features stark in the moonlight. "Anthony lied to us, Natalie. He tricked us both. He deliberately set out to keep us apart."

"Because we let him," she said sadly. "Because we didn't trust each other enough."

"Maybe. But we hadn't known each other that long, and it's hard to trust when someone like Anthony is feeding on your insecurities. He won. He got what he wanted. He broke us apart and kept us that way for seven long years." He paused, his hand reaching out to whisper against her hair. "The question now is, are we going to let him keep winning?"

Natalie's heart stopped at the look in his eyes. She shivered as he drew the back of his hand down her cheek. Her eyes drifted closed. Oh, how she relished his touch! Craved it with all her heart and soul. How she wanted him as she had never wanted anyone else.

"Spence—"

His fingertip trailed across her lips, silencing her. Gently he removed her glasses and set them aside. Then he pulled her to him, cupping her face with his hands as he feathered kisses along her jawline, drawing a deep shudder from her.

"There's still so much you don't know," she murmured, trying to steel her resolve, but failing. "I have to tell you something. Before it's too late."

Spence drew back and gazed into her eyes. "Does it have to do with Anthony?"

"Yes—"

"Then I don't want to hear it," he said.

"But you have to know—"

"The past is over, Natalie. At least for now. This moment belongs to us."

"But—"

This time he silenced her with his mouth. Natalie's lips opened instantly for him, and their tongues touched and mingled as thrill after thrill pulsed through her.

She squeezed her eyes closed, wrapping her arms around him and holding him close, knowing that at any moment, what she was feeling could be torn away from her. She'd learned the hard way that nothing lasts forever, and if she could have even one moment of happiness, one moment of the exquisite desire Spence unleashed inside her, she would be a fool not to take it.

He kissed her, whispered to her, touched her everywhere until her whole body ignited with passion. When he would have pulled away, she drew him back for another kiss, whispering to him, caressing him until she could feel his heart hammering beneath her hand on his chest—until she knew he wanted her as much as she wanted him.

Lips still meshed, fingers busy with their clothing, they began a slow dance toward the bedroom. Moonlight cascaded through the window, shadowing Spence's face as he stared down at her. Natalie shivered at the dark intensity in his eyes, knowing what was about to happen, yearning for it, and yet wishing, somehow, that this moment could be preserved forever.

"You're the only man I've ever wanted," she told him shyly. "I want you to know that."

His eyes softened, and he smiled at her so tenderly Natalie wanted to weep. He sat down on the bed and held out his hand. Without hesitation, she took it, allowing herself to be drawn once again into the thrilling warmth of his arms.

Chapter Thirteen

"Do you think anyone can tell?"

It was the next morning, and they were seated at a table near the river, having breakfast before Natalie went to work. She looked around at the half-dozen or so other diners scattered about the terrace, certain that every one of them would be able to tell by looking at her face what she and Spence had been up to last night. And this morning.

She glanced at him and smiled shyly, her gaze adoring his every feature.

Spence leaned across the table toward her, his eyes deepening to the color of the river. "If you keep looking at me like that, everyone will know, because I won't be able to keep my hands off you."

He touched her leg beneath the table, and a thrill raced up Natalie's spine. Images of last night danced in her head, drawing a blush to her cheeks. Their lovemaking had been so amazingly...*intimate.* She'd never dreamed that the touch of his lips behind her knee or the sound of his whisper in her ear could elicit such erotic sensations.

She'd never dreamed that she could be so uninhibited, so...*wanton.*

As Natalie sipped her coffee, she tried not to think about the consequences last night could bring. She tried not to think about the future at all, but it was there, looming before her, casting a dark shadow on the ray of happiness being with Spence had brought her.

As if sensing her unease, he said softly, "Try to relax, Natalie. It'll all be over soon."

She sighed. "I hope you're right. But what if Russo doesn't call? What if he gives up on the diamonds? You said yourself if he skipped town, the police would still need someone to pin Anthony's murder on."

"Russo isn't going to skip town." Slowly he picked up his coffee cup while he scanned the surroundings. His expression was one of casual interest, but Natalie knew that, like herself, he was anything but relaxed. He wanted to make sure everything was going according to plan, that all the agents were in place and every contingency had been covered.

The green eyes swept back to her. "He needs those diamonds. He'll call and set up the drop. When he does, we'll have him."

And this nightmare will finally be over, Natalie thought. But there were no guarantees and she knew it. Any number of things could go wrong. Russo might get cold feet and flee the country. He might get wind of the FBI's surveillance. And even if he were caught with the diamonds, the police might still refuse to drop their charges against her.

And Spence . . . might find out the truth.

After he had fallen asleep last night, Natalie had remained awake until the wee hours of the morning, thinking about all the lies that Anthony had told to keep them apart. And there was yet another lie between them. A lie that might tear asunder the fragile bond they had only just begun to mend last night.

Natalie closed her eyes briefly, wishing that she could tell Spence everything, but she'd kept the secret too well hidden for too many years. She'd protected her son for so long, the instinct was deeply ingrained in her being.

The truth was, she was afraid to tell him. Afraid of what he might do. She couldn't bear it if he aligned himself against her with Irene.

Natalie knew that if she didn't tell him, he would go back to Washington when all this was over. He would get on with his life, and she would get on with hers. The years loomed before her, bleak and lonely, but safe.

If she told Spence the truth, he might remain in San Antonio, but he might also demand more than Natalie was willing to give.

Suddenly, she didn't know which prospect was more frightening—a life with him or a life without him.

"Natalie?"

She glanced up.

"Are you all right?" His eyes burned into hers, and Natalie wondered suddenly what he would say if he knew what she was thinking. What he would do.

It was that question that had tormented her as Spence had lain sleeping beside her this morning. What would he do if he found out the truth?

"I'm fine," she said, but she could tell by the look in his eyes that he didn't believe her.

His hand slipped over hers. "You're thinking about Kyle, aren't you?"

She nodded, not trusting herself to speak.

"I won't let anything happen to him. You have my word."

"What about your mother?" she whispered. "Can you keep her from taking him away from me?"

Spence glanced away, running his hand through his dark hair. "I can only imagine how her threat must make you feel. If Kyle were my son..."

Her heart stopped as her eyes met his.

His gaze hardened. "If Kyle were my son, I'd do the same thing you are. I'd fight anyone who tried to take him away from me."

NATALIE WORKED IN HER shop all day, waiting on the few customers who drifted in, but she was ever mindful of the clock, the silent telephone, and Spence, waiting out of sight in her workroom.

The workroom door was open and Natalie could hear Spence and the female agent, who had already been inside the shop when they'd arrived that morning, talking in low voices. When the bells over the door chimed, signaling a customer, the sounds from the back room immediately ceased, only to start up again the moment the customer left.

Natalie wondered what they were talking about, but neither of them seemed inclined to draw her into their confidence. Even though they were in her shop, she was the outsider, and Natalie didn't much like it.

Agent Dianne Skelley was one of those women who had been born to intimidate other women. She was about the same height as Natalie, same fair skin, same light brown hair, but the resemblance ended there. Where Natalie was slender, almost reed-thin, Dianne Skelley was full-breasted and long-legged, with big, brown eyes and lush, full lips. *Ripe* was the word that came to mind. She carried herself with an air of supreme self-confidence that Natalie could only admire.

The very air around her seemed charged with electricity.

And to make matters worse, she was a toucher, at least as far as Spence was concerned. She was constantly taking his arm, touching his hand, finding a million-and-one ways to come into physical contact with him. They were on a first-name basis, and judging by the familiar way they worked together, Natalie couldn't help wondering if they'd once been something more.

She frowned, not liking the direction of her thoughts. She didn't like feeling jealous, but there it was. Spence had barely glanced at her since they'd arrived at the shop to find Agent Skelley waiting for them, and Natalie couldn't help but resent the way the agent now had his undivided attention, or the way she seemed to have completely taken over Natalie's workroom, turning it into a temporary surveillance-and-monitoring headquarters without so much as a word.

From her position by the counter, Natalie still couldn't make out what the two of them were saying back there, but she'd glanced inside the workroom a time or two, only to quickly retreat. The sophisticated-looking equipment was daunting enough, but the sight of those two heads bent together in cozy conspiracy was a little more than she could take.

Natalie told herself she should be glad Spence had such a compelling distraction at the moment. Because if he didn't, he might start to wonder about her reaction earlier at the restaurant, when he'd told her that if Kyle were his son, he would fight anyone who tried to take him away. He might start to wonder why she had looked so stunned by his revelation when his words had undoubtedly been uttered in sympathy.

He might start to wonder about a lot of things, and Natalie wasn't at all sure she was ready for explanations.

Needing to touch base with her son, she picked up the phone, hoping that talking to Kyle might alleviate some of her worries.

When she got him on the line, they chatted for several minutes about his day, about the cookies he'd made with his grandmother that morning and the game of Chinese checkers he'd played with his grandfather that afternoon.

Toward the end of the conversation, Natalie brought up the subject of the ivory comb she'd found in his treasure chest the night before, and how it had come to be in his possession.

"I didn't steal it, Mom, honest," he rushed to assure her. "I found it."

"Found it where?"

Kyle hesitated for a long moment, then said, "In my dad's office."

"*What?*" How had Blanche's antique comb ended up in Anthony's office? "Kyle, are you sure about that?"

"I promise," he said. "I was looking for my silver dollar Grandpa gave me, and I found it under a cushion on Dad's couch. He said it was just a piece of trash and he threw it away."

"If he threw it away, how did you come to have it?"

There was another long silence, then, "When he wasn't looking, I dug it out of the trash can," Kyle admitted. "But that's not the same thing as stealing, is it? He threw it away. He didn't want it."

Natalie didn't want to get into a discussion with a six-year-old about the ethics of going through someone else's trash can. She was still too shocked by what he'd told her. "What did you want with that comb, anyway, Kyle?"

"I thought it was pretty," he said in a quiet voice, sensing Natalie's displeasure with him. "I wanted to give it to you for Christmas. Are you mad at me, Mom? Did I do something bad?"

Natalie took a deep breath. "I'm not mad at you, honey. We'll talk about this later, okay?"

"Okay. When are you coming to get me? When can we go home?"

"Aren't you having a good time with Grandma and Grandpa?"

"Yeah, but . . . I wanna be with you."

"I want to be with you, too, sweetheart. And we will be. Very, very soon."

After a few more soothing words, Natalie hung up, then turned to find Spence standing in the workroom doorway, staring at her.

"What's wrong?" he asked.

"You remember the antique ivory comb I found in Kyle's tree house last night?" When he nodded, she said, "I told you it belonged to Blanche. Well, I just asked Kyle where he got it, and he said he found it in Anthony's office. But how could it have gotten there?"

"The answer seems pretty obvious. Blanche must have been there at one time or another."

"But she didn't even know Anthony," Natalie said.

"Are you sure about that?"

"Of course, I'm sure."

But as Natalie stood there relating her conversation with Kyle to Spence, her last meeting with Blanche came rushing back to her. The way Blanche had looked—as if she were deeply troubled about something. And then she'd admitted that the man she'd been seeing—the married man—had left her.

Naturally, Natalie had assumed her friend had meant that the man had dumped her. But, supposing Blanche had meant he'd left her *literally*? That he had died? And that the man had been Anthony?

Anthony and Blanche.

Natalie's heart flip-flopped inside her. Was it possible? And if so, why hadn't Blanche confided in her? Because she knew Natalie wouldn't approve? Or was it something else—something Natalie was afraid to even think about?

Had another friend betrayed her?

Although Natalie hadn't said anything for several seconds, Spence's thoughts must have been following hers exactly. He finally said, "Does Blanche have a key to this shop, Natalie?"

She looked up at him and nodded. "She offered to open up for me a few weeks ago when I had to take Kyle to the doctor. She has full-time help and I don't, so she said it was no big deal."

"She must have known the alarm code as well, then."

Again Natalie nodded.

"It's always puzzled me how Anthony was able to get in here the night he died without setting off the alarm. There was no sign of a forced entry. The police assumed that you had let him in, but—"

"I didn't," Natalie said. "So someone else must have."

"Exactly."

Blanche and Anthony. The names were like a litany inside Natalie's head. Had Blanche given Anthony the key to Natalie's store? Did Blanche know about the diamonds? Was she the one who had come in behind Natalie and—

She cut off her thoughts, reluctant to take them to the next step, not wanting to believe that Blanche had betrayed her, just as Melinda had once done.

But what if she had? What if Blanche knew something about the murder, but had deliberately withheld it from the police to implicate Natalie?

But why? What could she hope to gain—except perhaps her own freedom—if she were the one who had killed Anthony?

Spence turned to explain the situation to Agent Skelley, who lurked just behind him in the workroom. "Get someone up there to talk to Blanche Jones," he said. "I want to know where she was the night my brother was killed."

"We're not investigating Anthony's murder," Skelley objected. "That's the local P.D.'s jurisdiction."

"I'm making it mine," Spence said.

Skelley's elegant eyebrows drew together in a deep scowl. "Friend of yours or not, Sergeant Phillips will have a conniption if he finds out we've been interrogating suspects behind his back, not to mention withholding evidence."

Spence muttered something Natalie didn't quite catch, but by the look on Agent Skelley's face, it wasn't something she would want him to repeat.

"What about Washington?" Skelley challenged. "We have our assignment."

"And I'm broadening the parameters," Spence retorted. "Any problem with that?"

Their gazes clashed for the longest moment, and Natalie caught her breath at the look on Spence's face.

Never had she seen him look so determined. Or so dangerous.

Finally, Agent Skelley shrugged, backing down. She reached for the phone, and Natalie was left facing Spence, shivering at the dark look of triumph in his eyes.

A chilling thought rocked through her. She would hate to have him for an enemy. Spence wasn't afraid to break a few rules when it suited him.

Like all the other Bishops, he did whatever was necessary to win.

THE CALL FROM RUSSO—or at least the man they believed to be Russo—came just as Natalie was closing up shop that night. She glanced at Spence who nodded as he picked up the extension in the workroom. Natalie knew the call was being traced, just as every call that had come in that day had been.

Her fingers were shaking as she gripped the phone, recognizing Russo's gruff voice immediately. He got right to the point.

"For your sake, I hope you've decided to cooperate," he said.

"You left me little choice," Natalie said, hoping her statement didn't sound as practiced to Russo as it did to her. If he guessed that she had been coached, the natural assumption would be that she had gone to the police, and Natalie shuddered to think what Russo would do in that case. "If I give you the diamonds, what assurance do I have that you'll leave my son and me alone?"

There was a pause, then Russo laughed softly, a sound that sent deep chills up Natalie's spine. "If you give me the diamonds, what reason would I have to kill you? Pleasure?"

Yes, Natalie thought, shuddering. A man like Russo would probably take a great deal of pleasure in killing. Maybe that was why he'd killed Anthony.

"At least give me your word," Natalie said, trying to hold him on the phone for as long as she could.

Another laugh. "All right," he said. "You have my word. But if you double-cross me, if I see a cop within a mile of you, your son's as good as dead. Understand?"

Natalie gripped the phone even tighter. "I understand," she whispered.

"There's a pay phone at the corner of Houston and Alamo," Russo said. "You have fifteen minutes to get there."

The phone clicked and the line went dead. On shaky legs, Natalie went to the doorway of the workroom. Spence was talking softly on the phone, but his gaze was on her.

"Did you get a trace?"

"A pay phone," Agent Skelley said. "On Commerce."

"Get the area staked out," Spence said, checking the clip on his weapon.

Both of them looked keyed up, wired, ready to move, but Natalie's words stopped them.

"I think I should be the one to go," she said.

Identical expressions of exasperation crossed Skelley's and Spence's features. Spence said, "We've been through this, Natalie. It's too dangerous."

"But why should she have to take my place?" Natalie demanded, glancing at Skelley who had changed into a sweater and skirt identical to hers. The agent had even combed the curls out of her light brown hair in imitation of Natalie's more casual style.

Spence said, "Agent Skelley's been through rigorous training. She knows the risks."

Skelley shrugged, as if the danger she was about to face was inconsequential.

The easy thing would be to sit back and let her do it, Natalie thought. She had no wish to play heroine, but she would do whatever was necessary to protect her son. If Russo suspected a trap, he might go straight for Kyle.

She said as much to Spence. He glanced at Skelley. "Wait for me outside. I'll just be a minute."

Skelley rolled her eyes as she walked by, giving him a look that clearly said, *Where did you get her?*

Spence closed the door behind Skelley, then turned and placed his hands on Natalie's arms. "You have to trust me. I know what I'm doing. We all do."

"But if it doesn't work... If he suspects a trap..."

"He won't," Spence said. "Agent Skelley's an expert at this, believe me. She could fool her own mother if she had to, and as far as we know, Russo has never seen you up close. It'll work."

"And if it doesn't?" Natalie challenged.

"It will." He bent and kissed her quickly. "Keep the door locked and stay out of sight. I'll let you know as soon as there's news."

TIME CRAWLED. Natalie lost count of how many times she'd glanced at her watch. She couldn't help worrying that something had gone wrong. Her imagination went wild, thinking up the worst possible scenarios. What if the plan hadn't worked? What if Russo smelled a trap and opened fire? What if Spence had gotten hurt or... worse?

Stop it! she ordered herself. *Don't borrow trouble.*

Finally, just to occupy her mind, Natalie got up and started straightening her workroom. Frank's "boys," as he'd called the young men who had cleaned up the room, hadn't known what to do with some of the boxes and packing material she'd had stored on the shelves, so they'd stacked them all in a corner. Natalie began to put all the materials away.

Finishing that, she dusted her hands and glanced around, wondering what she could do now. Her eyes fell on the asparagus fern hanging in the small window behind her desk, and she realized she couldn't remember the last time she'd watered it. Filling a pitcher from the bathroom, Natalie pulled a stepladder over to the window and climbed up, feeling the soil with her fingers to determine dryness.

Suddenly her hand touched something solid, and her first instinct was to recoil at the unknown. Then her curiosity got the better of her, and she lifted the item from the pot, staring down at the little black tape recorder she held in her hand.

Natalie recognized it immediately. It was the one Anthony had given to Kyle, the one she'd asked her son to return, only he'd said he couldn't find it. A small fabrication, to say the least. Natalie remembered the day Kyle had come back to the workroom to get his teacher's present. Later, she'd noticed the stepladder had been pulled over to the fern, but she'd assumed Michelle had used it to water the plant. Now Natalie realized that Kyle must have climbed up on the ladder and hidden the recorder in the fern, so Natalie wouldn't make him give it back to his father.

She studied the controls for a moment. The recorder was voice activated, and the tape was all the way to the end. Natalie rewound, then pushed the Play button. Her own voice startled her in the deep quiet of the shop. The beginning was chopped off, while the recorder activated itself, then her voice came in loud and clear. She was talking to Michelle, issuing a string of instructions before rushing out on an errand. The next sound, again chopped at the very beginning, came from Michelle. She was talking on the telephone, obviously to her boyfriend.

So much for following instructions, Natalie thought dryly.

She reached down and fast-forwarded the tape. Again she heard her own voice, this time talking on the phone to a supplier, then to a courier, making arrangements for a package to be picked up and delivered.

Natalie was about to fast-forward again, when the significance of the last conversation hit her, slamming her heart against her chest. She had been making arrangements for *Anthony's* package to be picked up. The tape recorder had been turned on the day of Anthony's murder. Kyle had hidden it late that afternoon. And if it had been recording that day...what about that night?

Her hands shaking, Natalie sat down at her desk and listened to another phone conversation, then another before fast-forwarding once again. Suddenly, her breath suspended in her throat as she heard the voice she'd been searching for. She rewound for just an instant, then pressed Play.

"...are they?" Anthony's voice demanded.

Her own voice, sounding shocked, asked, "What are you doing here? How did you get in?"

Natalie heard herself gasp on the tape as Anthony grabbed her arm. Memories of that night came crashing in on her. She remembered how surprised she'd been to see Anthony in her shop, then afraid because of the way he was acting. She'd never seen him look so desperate, so out of control. Now Natalie understood why. The diamonds were missing and he must have known Russo would come after him.

"What the hell do you think you're doing?" her voice demanded on the tape.

"Where are they, Natalie?"

"I don't know what you're talking about, but I'm calling the police. Even you can't get away with this, Anthony."

There was a hesitation, as Anthony pulled the phone jack out of the wall, then, "You found them, didn't you?" A crash, as he threw the phone against the wall. "You thought you could pull a fast one on me, didn't you? You've always been just a little too clever for your own good, Natalie. But not this time. Now hand them over before I do something we might both regret—"

Natalie remembered how he had glanced over her shoulder as someone came up behind her. "What are you doing he—"

She gasped as the sound of her body crashing to the floor came over the tape. Her whole being tensed as she leaned forward, staring at the little black box on her desk. Whose voice would she hear next? The murderer's?

"What the hell did you do that for?" Anthony demanded on the tape. Another silence, then, "She's still breathing. You're damned lucky you didn't kill her."

A second or two went by, during which the only sounds Natalie heard were background noises as someone moved about the workroom. Then Anthony's voice, taunting, said, "What were you doing, following me? Did you think I'd come here for an assignation with my ex-wife?" He laughed—a mean, nasty sound that chilled Natalie to the bone. "Were you hoping to watch?"

The response was a low, garbled sound, like someone in pain. Then Anthony laughed again and said, "Look at her. Even unconscious, she's twice the woman you are. Did you really think you could take her place? You're nothing more than a high-priced call girl."

There was another sound of protest, then almost in a whisper the woman spoke for the first time, and Natalie's heart stopped for a painful second as she recognized the voice on the tape. The voice of Anthony's killer.

"Do you know how much I hate you?" Melinda whispered. "How much I hate *her?*"

"I have some idea," Anthony answered, unconcerned. "How did you get in here, anyway?"

"The same way you did," Melinda replied. "With a key. For someone who thinks he's so smart, you can be awfully stupid, Anthony, leaving your keys lying around for your wife to find and duplicate. I have keys to your car, to your office, to your private files, and to that cozy little apartment you share with your mistress. You didn't know I knew about her, did you? Sleeping with Natalie's best friend. Couldn't you be a little more original, darling?"

She must have gotten his attention with that, because Anthony's voice lost its mocking edge. He said grimly, "You never answered my question, Melinda. What are you doing here?"

"I've come to kill you," she said. It was Melinda's turn to laugh, and she did so, with gusto, obviously relishing having the upper hand for once. "You didn't really think I'd let you walk out on me, did you? Not after everything I've done for you, you bastard."

"Where did you get that gun?" Anthony asked. His voice sounded strained, unnatural, as if he were striving for a calmness he was far from feeling.

"From your office." The mirth had disappeared from Melinda's voice, and she sounded grim now, completely resolved. "It's registered to Natalie. You bought it for her right after the two of you were married, remember? She told me all about it, how she despised guns and wouldn't have it in the house so you took it away. Everyone forgot all about it, but I didn't. I knew you still had it, and now, when I kill you, everyone will think Natalie did it. She'll go to prison for your murder. It's too perfect."

"It *is* too perfect," Anthony agreed. "Too clever by far for you to have dreamed up all by yourself."

"I'm a lot smarter than you ever gave me credit for," Melinda retorted angrily.

"No, you're not," Anthony said. "You're just a stupid little nobody who would stab her own mother in the back if the price was right—"

Suddenly, Melinda screamed as something crashed to the floor, followed by definite sounds of a struggle. Then Anthony, breathing hard, said, "You stupid little fool. Did you really think you could pull that trigger? You haven't got the guts or the gumption—" His voice cut off sharply on a gasp, as if he'd been taken by surprise.

Then another voice—a voice Natalie thought she recognized—said, "She may not have the guts or the gumption to kill you, but I do."

Anthea? Natalie thought in disbelief.

Anthony gasped again and groaned—a low, animal sound that sent chill after chill pulsing through Natalie. A loud thud followed, presumably his body falling to the floor, and Natalie's hand flew to her mouth as she realized she'd just heard the sounds of Anthony's murder on tape. Her heart flailed against her chest as she closed her eyes tightly, trying to fight the nausea rising inside her.

Then Melinda screamed, drawing Natalie's attention back to the tape. Anthea said harshly, "Shut up, you idiot. We've got work to do. You very nearly cost us everything."

Definitely Anthea, Natalie thought.

"It wasn't my fault," Melinda whined. "He jumped me and took the gun away from me—"

"Shut up," Anthea ordered. "And help me move Natalie over here, near the body. Put the knife in her hand."

Natalie was shocked to hear herself groan in protest on the tape.

"Hurry!" Anthea urged. "She's coming around. We'll call 911 from the pay phone downstairs—"

There were more sounds of frenzied activity and then in the background, a door closed softly. Then everything was silent.

Natalie, her heart pounding, stared at the tape, thinking that it was all over. She'd heard everything, but then the recorder had been activated again, and Anthony, gasping, struggling for breath, said, "Natalie...not...the one. Natalie...not you...not you..."

It was the same thing he'd been whispering when the police had arrived to find Natalie, murder weapon in hand, kneeling over him. "Natalie...not you..."

The police, of course, had interpreted that as a dying man's accusation, pointing the finger at his murderer, when in actuality, Anthony had been trying to clear her.

Natalie sat stunned by the revelations she'd heard on that tape. When she looked up, there was a shadow in the doorway—tall, thin, with short black hair slicked back . . .

Chapter Fourteen

For a moment, Natalie thought it was Anthony who stared across the room at her, and then, with a painful plunging of her heart, she realized it was Anthea. Anthea, dressed in black trousers and a black turtleneck, the masculine clothing adding to the ghostly illusion. Anthea, holding a gun leveled at Natalie.

In spite of the weapon, she looked as stunned as Natalie felt. Her eyes were glued to the tape recorder, which was still running. Loud voices sprang from the tape—police officers ordering Natalie to drop the knife and move away from the body, Natalie's stuttered responses to their questions, and then Anthony whispering into the hushed silence one last time, "Natalie...not you..."

Slowly, taking care to make no sudden moves, Natalie lifted her finger and pushed the Stop button. Anthea was still standing in the doorway, but now the stunned look had left her face to be replaced by one of anger. She advanced toward Natalie and held out her hand.

"I'll take that tape."

When Natalie hesitated, Anthea said, "After listening to that, do you doubt I would pull this trigger?"

Natalie shook her head, her eyes on Anthea, but her mind was casting about frantically for a weapon or a means of escape. Unfortunately, she seemed to be trapped.

She placed the recorder in Anthea's hand. Quickly, Anthea ejected the tape, slipped it in her pocket, then placed the recorder on Natalie's desk. For the first time, Natalie realized Anthea was wearing gloves, and that— perhaps even more than the gun—brought home the woman's sinister intent.

Anthea motioned with the gun. "Get your car keys," she ordered. "Nice and slow. We're going for a little drive."

"Why should I go with you?" Natalie asked, her heart pounding like a piston inside her. "You obviously intend to kill me. Why should I make it easier for you?"

"Because if you don't," Anthea said matter-of-factly, "I'll shoot you dead where you stand. Now, get the keys."

Natalie knew Anthea meant what she said. In either case, her chances didn't look good, but at least, if she went with Anthea, she would be buying herself a little more time.

Natalie removed her purse from her desk drawer and fished for her keys. She held them up, and Anthea grabbed them out of her hand.

"Let's go."

As Natalie walked ahead of Anthea into the shop, her gaze went automatically to the front door, praying that Spence would walk through at that moment...and praying that he wouldn't. Anthea had already killed one brother. There was no reason to believe she wouldn't kill another.

As if reading her mind, Anthea said, "Spence won't be coming to save you, if that's what you're hoping. In fact, he may not be coming back at all."

Natalie glanced over her shoulder. "What do you mean?"

"He's walking into an ambush," Anthea said and smiled. "A setup. Russo knows the feds are on to him, and he's laid a little trap of his own."

Natalie gasped, her heart tripping in fear. "You told him?"

"Just like I tipped the FBI to the fact that Anthony was holding the diamonds. Men are so stupid," Anthea added in disgust. "None of them have a clue."

"But you do," Natalie said, forcing an admiring note into her voice. "I always thought you were the clever Bishop. Smarter by far than Anthony."

"Stuff it," Anthea retorted, jabbing the gun into Natalie's ribs. "You're not going to get anywhere by trying to keep me talking."

They were outside now, going down the steps. Anthea was right beside Natalie, holding her arm. Natalie could feel the gun poking against her side as they descended the steps together.

"Where are we going?" Natalie asked, her gaze scanning the surroundings.

"Just keep walking."

It was late and a weeknight, so the Riverwalk was deserted, the restaurants and shops having long since closed. Natalie wondered if she should try to break away and make a run for it, but, as if sensing her intention, Anthea tightened her grip—as strong as any man's—on Natalie's arm.

They ascended the concrete steps to the parking area, where Natalie's car was parked. The right rear fender was still smashed in, where she and Kyle had been rammed the day of Anthony's funeral. She wondered now if Anthea had had something to do with that, as well.

Anthea released Natalie's arm long enough to unlock the passenger door, and then, after some difficulty, opened it. She made Natalie slide in first and get behind the wheel, then Anthea climbed in and slammed the door. She handed Natalie the keys. "Let's go."

"Where to?" Natalie inserted the key into the ignition. She prayed the car wouldn't start, but the engine turned over on the first crank.

"You'll find out soon enough." Anthea motioned with the gun for Natalie to head out of the parking lot.

They drove for fifteen or twenty minutes, taking Broadway away from downtown. They passed the zoo and the Japanese Tea Garden with its sky tram and took a back street to a remote area of the park. And all the while Natalie's thoughts were on Kyle. She had to find a way to protect him, to save him from Russo.

And Spence. *Dear God, please let him be all right,* she prayed. What if she lost both Kyle and Spence? What if she never got the chance to tell them the truth?

At Anthea's direction, Natalie pulled the car to the side of the road and parked. They both got out, and Anthea took Natalie's arm and steered her through the dense forest of cypress trees and water oaks toward the river.

"Just tell me one thing," Natalie said, as they neared the water. "If you had all this planned, why did you try to bribe me to leave town that day?"

"Because I would have followed you," Anthea said, as if she couldn't believe Natalie hadn't figured it out for herself. "It would have been so much easier to get rid of you and the kid away from here, away from all the suspicions. You would have just disappeared, and no one would ever have known. But you wouldn't go and so now I'll just have to be patient.''

"What do you mean?" Natalie stumbled over a dead branch, and Anthea grabbed her arm roughly.

"Anthony's dead, Spence is walking into an ambush, and you're about to commit suicide. That leaves just one person standing in my way."

"Kyle," Natalie breathed.

"The kid will have to wait awhile," Anthea said. "Though, after you're gone, Mother will undoubtedly get custody. That'll make an...unfortunate accident so much easier to arrange.''

Natalie's heart pounded in terror. She had to find a way out of here. She had to protect Kyle.

But how could she get away? Anthea had a death grip on her arm.

Melinda was waiting for them by the river. She stood shivering in the moonlight, her arms wrapped around her middle as she watched them approach.

Natalie turned to Anthea. "Why did you bring me here?"

"I told you," Anthea said. "You're about to commit suicide.''

"Poor thing," Melinda cooed. "You've been so distraught. Overcome with guilt for what you did. The idea of facing a trial and then life in prison is too much for you. You simply can't go on."

"No one will believe that," Natalie argued, her heart racing as fast as her mind. She had to get out of here. Now. Before it was too late. She had to make sure Kyle was safe, and she had to somehow get to Spence—if he was still alive.

"The police will believe it. After all, they already think you're a murderer." Anthea waved the gun at their surroundings. "It's pretty isolated out here. It may take a couple of days for them to find your body. By that time, the D.A. will have received your suicide note in the mail."

Moonlight gleamed in Anthea's eyes, but what Natalie saw wasn't madness. It was greed. It was hate. And it was triumph.

Melinda glanced around uneasily. "Let's get on with it," she said. "It's creepy out here."

"You'll never get away with it," Natalie said, desperate now to stall the inevitable.

"We already have gotten away with it," Anthea said. "I've been planning this for a long, long time, every last detail. I even planted the custody papers in Anthony's office, so the police would think you had a motive to kill him. I've thought of everything. Nothing can go wrong now."

"What about the tape?" Natalie said quickly. "You didn't plan on that, did you?"

Momentary doubt flashed in Anthea's eyes. Melinda said, "What tape?"

When Anthea didn't answer, Natalie did, "There was a tape recorder in my office the night Anthony was killed. The murder…everything was captured on tape."

Melinda gasped. "Is that true, Anthea?"

Anthea shrugged. "I have the tape now, so what difference does it make?"

"I made a copy," Natalie said.

Melinda swore viciously, but Anthea just shook her head. "She's lying. I saw her face. She was as surprised by that tape as I was. There's no copy. Is there?"

She sneered at Natalie, daring her to try and make a run for it.

"The point is," Natalie said, striving to keep the fear and desperation out of her voice, "you didn't plan for that tape. What else might you have missed? What else is out there that will give you two away?"

"You said nothing could go wrong," Melinda whined. "You said everything would go according to plan. You said if we stuck together, we'd get it all. With Anthony and Spence gone and Natalie dead or in prison, the only person standing in our way would be Kyle. You said you'd take care of him, when the time was right. You said—"

"Shut up!" Anthea whirled around, turning the gun on Melinda. "Shut up, you whining bitch!"

Melinda's eyes widened in the moonlight. Natalie could see the fear on her face as she said urgently, "If you shoot me, what happens to your alibi for the night Anthony was murdered? Or tonight, for that matter? We're in this together, Anthea. You need me just as much as I need you."

As Natalie listened to the conspirators argue, she edged back, one tiny step at a time, toward the woods. Then, taking a deep breath, she whirled to run, diving headlong for cover. Melinda screamed a warning. Anthea turned and fired just as Natalie's foot caught a tree root and she fell sprawling to the ground. The bullet whizzed over her head and slammed into a tree trunk, the sound reverberating across the river.

Half crawling, half running, Natalie scrambled toward the woods, but Anthea was right behind her. "Stop right there," she said in a voice filled with deadly intent, "or I'll shoot you in the back."

Natalie hesitated, then turned.

"Face it, Natalie. There's no way out for you."

"You won't get away with this," Natalie whispered again.

Anthea shrugged. "I'm a Bishop. I can get away with anything. And once this tape is destroyed—" she pulled the tape from her pocket and held it up in the moonlight "—no one will ever know who killed Anthony. Or you. I'll have everything I ever wanted. Money, power, and—"

"Mother's undying devotion," said a voice from the darkness. "That's really why you did it, isn't it, Anthea?"

In unison, Natalie and Anthea swung toward the sound. Spence came out of the woods and faced his sister. "It's over, Anthea. Give me the tape."

Natalie stared at his dark profile, relief flooding through her. He was all right!

While sister and brother stared at each other, Melinda tried to make a run for it, but someone else emerged from the woods and caught her, holding her fast. Melinda struggled for a moment, then dropped to her knees, sobbing hysterically.

"She made me do it!" she screamed. "It was all her idea!"

"Shut up!" Anthea whirled toward Melinda. "Keep your mouth shut, you idiot!"

In a flash, Spence grabbed Anthea's arm and wrenched away the gun. The tape went flying through the air. For one breathless moment Natalie thought it would fall into the water, and the evidence that would clear her would be forever lost. But the tape landed on the bank, mere inches from the river. She walked over and picked it up. Her hand trembling, she clutched it to her breast.

Spence turned back to Anthea. "That's why you killed him, isn't it? You wanted Mother's love. With Anthony gone, you thought she would turn to you."

Anthea said nothing, but Melinda couldn't seem to keep her mouth shut. It was as if a dam had burst wide open. "Yes! *She* killed him! And she threatened to kill me if I didn't go along with her. Look at her! Look at the way she's dressed. She's a flaming psychopath. Half the time, she thinks she *is* Anthony. That's why she killed him, so she could take his place!"

The whole bizarre circle now focused on Melinda. As if aware that this could well be the performance of a lifetime, she dissolved into tears once again. "You have to believe me, Spence," she sobbed. "It was all her idea, and she frightened me into helping her. I didn't want to do it. I loved Anthony!" Melinda would have collapsed to the ground again if not for the man who was holding her up, the man Natalie now recognized as Frank Delmontico.

"You're lying," Anthea said, defending herself at last. "You wanted him dead as much as I did."

"No! I loved him—"

"You wanted him dead because he wanted a divorce. He despised you. He still loved Natalie and you knew it."

"He never loved her—"

Once her own flood started, Anthea couldn't seem to stem it. The words gushed from her mouth, frothing with venom. "The only reason he married you was to spite her. He hated you from the very first. He told me he couldn't stand to look at you, touch you. That the only way he could...perform in bed was to pretend you were her.''

Natalie's skin crawled as she listened to the two of them fight. She could only imagine what Spence must be feeling. She glanced at his face, but all she saw was darkness and shadow.

Dimly, Natalie became aware of other people moving in from the woods, police officers surrounding the clearing. But Melinda and Anthea seemed not to notice. They were too intent on blaming the other, too bent on destroying each other.

"You hated him because he loved her," Anthea taunted again.

Then, suddenly, Melinda seemed to snap. She screamed as if mortally wounded, and tore her hands through her hair. "Yes, I hated him! I hated him for what he did to me! I wanted him dead. All these years he let me think I was the one who couldn't have children. He called me barren, empty, half a woman when all the time *he* was the one. He was sterile, and he didn't tell me. He let the whole world think it was me!''

Her words fell like bombs in the stillness of the night. Natalie gasped as their meaning struck her. She felt Spence's eyes on her in the darkness, but she didn't turn and look at him. She couldn't.

"What about Kyle?" Spence asked, although Natalie had no idea to whom he was addressing the question.

"Take a wild guess," Melinda replied. "He can't be Anthony's."

"Is this true?"

Natalie glanced up. Although she couldn't see his face in the darkness, she could feel the power of his eyes on her. Those Bishop eyes. Eyes so like his son's.

"Is it true?" he asked again.

But before Natalie could speak, Spence turned and walked away.

Chapter Fifteen

Natalie watched numbly as Melinda and Anthea were handcuffed and led away by the officers. Frank Delmontico came over to her and handed her his jacket.

"It's cold out here," he said.

"Thanks," she mumbled, accepting the jacket and spreading it over her shoulders. It was colder than he could ever imagine, Natalie thought, fighting back tears.

"Are you ready to go?"

She looked up at him. "Go where?"

He shrugged. "The police station. I suspect we're all in for a long night."

For the first time, Frank's part in the night's events hit Natalie. She stared at him in the darkness. "What are you doing here, anyway?"

He shrugged again. "I still have a lot of friends on the street, and I heard what was going down tonight. Normally, I don't have a lot of use for the feds, but Russo—" His voice hardened. "That son of a bitch is the reason I spent ten years in prison. He framed me and I swore I'd find a way to get even with him. Tonight I got my chance."

Natalie looked at him in surprise. She'd never seen such passion in Frank Delmontico's eyes. "So you warned Spence about the ambush?"

"Damn straight, I warned him."

"What are you doing *here?*" she asked, waving her hand at their surroundings. "How did you and Spence know where to find me?"

"I've been watching you lately," Frank admitted. "Keeping my eye on you. I know what it's like to be accused of a crime you didn't commit. I thought maybe I could find a way to help you. When I saw you leave your shop with the Bishop woman, I figured she was up to no good. I tailed the two of you out to the parking lot where I hooked up with Spence. We followed you out here."

An ex-con and an FBI agent coming to her rescue. Yet another irony in her life, Natalie thought.

"How can I ever thank you," she said, putting her hand on Frank's sleeve.

He smiled grimly. "The only thanks I want is to see Jack Russo behind bars. And Spence has already promised me that pleasure."

AT POLICE HEADQUARTERS, Natalie gave her statement and was then ushered into a small holding room. Thanks to the tape, she'd been assured that the charges against her would be dropped immediately. Natalie knew she should be ecstatic that her nightmare was finally coming to an end, but she wasn't. All she could think about was Spence and the look on his face before he'd turned and walked away from her.

The door to the room opened, and she glanced up, hoping it would be Spence. But when Blanche walked through the door, Natalie's heart dropped. She wasn't ready to face her friend yet. Not after what she'd learned tonight.

Was that how Spence felt about her? she wondered.

Blanche looked terrible. She looked as if she'd dressed in a big hurry, throwing on the first thing she found and not bothering to comb her hair or put on makeup. She approached Natalie tentatively and sat down beside her.

"I can only imagine what you must think of me," she said quietly. "You must think I'm little better than Melinda."

"You're not a murderer," Natalie said.

"No. I'm not a murderer." Her voice was filled with self-loathing. "I'm just a stupid woman who betrayed her best friend. The only real friend I've ever had. Oh, Natalie." She broke down then, weeping softly into her hands. Finally she looked up, wiping the tears from her face with the back of her hand. "The only excuse I have is that I loved him," she whispered. "I really loved him."

"Then I'm sorry for you," Natalie said softly.

Blanche glanced away, as if no longer able to meet Natalie's eyes. "When he came to me and asked for the key and alarm code to your shop, I refused at first. I couldn't imagine why he wanted them. But he said you had something of his. Something you wouldn't give back. He only needed a few moments alone in your shop to find it, and then his relationship with you would be severed forever. I thought if he got what he wanted, he'd leave you and Kyle alone."

Natalie stared at her in disbelief. "Are you saying you did it for me?"

Blanche closed her eyes briefly. "I wish I could. But I was thinking of myself. I thought if I could help him do this one thing—"

"He would be grateful enough to leave Melinda and marry you."

Blanche nodded. "As I said before, I'm a stupid woman."

Natalie let that pass without comment. "After I was charged with Anthony's murder, when the police thought that I had let him into my shop, why didn't you come forward then? Why didn't you try to clear me?"

Blanche turned back to her. "I was afraid to! Don't you see? I had a motive every bit as strong as yours. The shunned, desperate mistress. I couldn't take that chance. I was too scared."

"And so you said nothing," Natalie said coldly. "What if I had been convicted? Would you still have remained silent?"

"I don't like to think so." Blanche stared down at her hands.

"But you don't know for sure, do you? I thought you were my friend, Blanche. I thought I could trust you."

Blanche lifted her tearstained face. "Can you ever forgive me?" she whispered.

"I don't know," Natalie answered sadly, her thoughts once again turning to Spence. "Sometimes forgiveness is not that easy to come by."

DAWN HAD BROKEN BEFORE Natalie finally saw Spence again. He came to the holding room to bring her home. For that small gesture, Natalie was profoundly grateful, because she knew what it had cost him. He had found out in the cruelest way possible that Kyle was his son, and Natalie had only herself to blame.

She glanced at his silent profile as he pulled the car into her parents' driveway and killed the engine. He sat for a moment with his arms draped over the steering wheel, looking indescribably weary as he gazed out at the dawn. It was all Natalie could do not to reach out to him.

Instead she remained silent, waiting for him to speak. When he turned to her, she held her breath.

"Why didn't you tell me?" he asked at last. "Back then, when you first found out. Why didn't you tell me?"

"You don't know how much I wanted to," Natalie told him. "But you were gone. I didn't even know how to find you. And then Anthony started telling me all those lies about you, making me believe that you had never cared about me, and that you certainly wouldn't want my baby. I was alone and I was frightened and I didn't know what to do."

"So you listened to Anthony."

Natalie sighed. "He told me that he would marry me and give my baby a name. He said it was the perfect solution for everyone concerned. The baby would be taken care of, and you would never have to know. You and your... fiancée could get married, just like you'd planned. No one had to get hurt."

"You said last night that by the time I came back, you'd already found out what kind of man Anthony was. Why didn't you tell me then?"

"Because by then Anthony had made me strike a bargain with him. He made me promise I would never tell anyone the baby wasn't his. He said medical tests could be faked and doctors could be paid to say anything that he wanted them to say. He said if I made trouble for him, he would prove in court that the baby was his, and that I was an unfit mother. He would take Kyle away from me, and I would never see him again. And I believed him," she said, wiping her moist cheek with the back of her hand. "I knew what he was capable of."

"So you said nothing," Spence said, unmoved by her tears. "And all these years, I've lived without my son."

"I'm sorry," Natalie whispered. "But back then, I'd gotten myself into such a mess with Anthony, I didn't see any other way out. All I could think about was protecting Kyle."

"What about after Anthony was dead?" Spence demanded. "What about last night, before we made love? Didn't you think I had a right to know then?"

"Yes. I wanted to tell you. I tried to tell you, but...so much has happened lately, to both of us. Anthony's murder, my arrest. And then your mother, threatening to take Kyle away from me. I... just didn't think the time was right."

"Would the time ever have been right?"

She turned away from his accusing eyes. "I... don't know."

"You didn't trust me, did you?"

"We didn't trust each other, and just like you once told me, I had to consider every possibility." Natalie wasn't looking at him, but she could feel his eyes on her, boring into her, drilling her with accusation. She turned to him, her gaze pleading for understanding. "Don't you see? Kyle means everything to me. I couldn't stand the thought of losing him. Without him—"

"Don't," Spence interrupted harshly. "Don't tell me how empty your life would be without him. Because I already know, Natalie. I already know how empty a life can be."

She had never seen eyes more bleak than Spence's at that moment. She had hurt him, more deeply than she had ever dreamed possible, and Natalie was very much afraid he would never be able to forgive her.

"Please try to see it from my point of view," she begged.

He shook his head. "I'm trying to, but all I seem to be able to think about is the last six years I've spent alone. It didn't have to be that way."

His features looked ravaged in the pale light of dawn, and Natalie could only imagine what this night had done to him.

"I'm sorry," she whispered again. "I'm so sorry."

"I'm sorry, too," he said, his eyes as hard as steel. "I'm sorry it ever had to come to this."

TWO DAYS LATER, on Christmas Eve, a cold front moved into the area, and the temperature dropped fifty degrees overnight. Suddenly the riverside tables along the Riverwalk were deserted, save for the blackbirds and pigeons who braved the cold weather to peck at a few stray bread crumbs.

Natalie stood at the front window of her shop, enjoying a lull in what had been an impossibly busy morning—thank goodness—as she stared down at the wind-tossed tree limbs overhanging the river. The last two days had been a whirlwind of activity. The charges against her had been dropped, and every newspaper and news station in the state seemed to be clamoring for a statement or an interview with her.

A picture of her and Kyle, beaming at each other, had made the front page yesterday. Right next to it, a photograph of a somber Spence leaving the courthouse after Anthea's arraignment had brought home to Natalie, once again, the differences in their circumstances. Her life was on the fast track back to normal, but Spence's life would never be the same. His brother had been killed and his sister was the murderer. How did one get over something like that? Natalie wondered, staring at the river. She had everything to be thankful for, and Spence . . .

Spence had nothing.

He has a son, she reminded herself. *He has me.*

But he doesn't want you.

And who could blame him? Spence's wounded voice echoed in Natalie's mind. *"What about last night, before we made love? Didn't you think I had a right to know then?"*

She closed her eyes. Yes, he'd had a right to know. She should have told him—almost had told him—but it wasn't something you could just blurt out. The time had to be right. Feelings had to be considered. Consequences had to be weighed.

At least, that was what she'd told herself.

"You didn't trust me, did you?"

She *hadn't* trusted him, Natalie realized. Not seven years ago, and not now. What did that say about her? she wondered. Why did she always allow herself to believe the very worst about Spence? About the man she loved?

Her heart thumped against her chest as the revelation hit her.

The man she loved.

She was in love with Spencer Bishop. Again. Still. She'd never stopped loving him. So why hadn't she told him? Why hadn't she told him everything when they were being so open with each other the night they'd made love?

Because she hadn't wanted to get hurt again, Natalie realized. Trusting someone completely was too risky. It meant putting yourself out there, giving as good as you got, and she'd never been quite willing to do that.

For the most part, Natalie had lived a charmed life. Her parents had loved her and protected her, but when things had gone wrong, she'd given up on Spence without so much as a question. She'd found it easier to believe Anthony's lies than to fight for the man she loved—because if she'd fought for him and lost, there would have been nothing left for her.

And what did she have now? Natalie asked herself with brutal honesty. She had Kyle and she had her parents, but she didn't have Spence; and for the first time in seven years, she let herself feel the devastation of that loss.

It was Christmas Eve and she was a free woman, but Natalie had never felt more miserable. Or more lonely.

SPENCE STOOD AT THE WALL of windows in the airport and watched the 747 ascend into the clouds. Irene was on her way to London for an extended visit with friends. She'd escaped from San Antonio and the flurry of publicity Anthea's and Melinda's arrests had stirred, leaving Spence behind to clean up the mess.

As far as he knew, Irene had not spoken to Natalie to apologize for her unjust accusations, nor had she alleviated Natalie's fears regarding her threat to take Kyle away. But Spence knew that was over. Once Irene had learned the truth about Kyle—that he was not Anthony's son, but Spence's—her interest in the boy had vanished, along with any pretense of concern for his welfare.

She was gone, possibly for good, and Spence wished he could find it in himself to care. But Irene had never been a mother to him, and it was too late to pretend they were anything more than strangers to each other.

He couldn't help comparing her to Natalie. Natalie adored Kyle, and she showed him in a thousand ways every single day just how much she loved him. Kyle would grow up secure in that love. He wouldn't have to look back on his childhood with the same bitter emptiness that Spence had always felt about his.

Whatever Natalie had done, whatever secrets she had kept, Spence knew, deep in his heart, that she had done so to protect their son. Everything had been for Kyle. If the situation had been reversed, Spence couldn't say for sure he wouldn't have done the same thing.

The question now was, where did that leave them? With all the lies and the secrets and the years that had gone by, was there anything left for them?

To be honest, Spence didn't know. But what he did know was that the thought of returning to Washington—to that bleak, empty apartment, to that cold, meaningless life—brought a stab of pain to his heart. He already felt lonesome for Natalie and Kyle and for what they might have built together.

But it was better for a man like him not to have ties, he reminded himself grimly. A family made you care too much, made you lose your edge. And that was a dangerous thing.

Better that he should go back to Washington and let Kyle and Natalie get on with their lives without him.

Better that he should go back to his own life and forget about what might have been.

"WHEN'S SANTA COMING?" Kyle asked, as he and Natalie finished wrapping the last of the presents. Natalie had closed the shop early that evening, and she and Kyle had been busy ever since they'd gotten home, trying to get everything ready for the next day.

The house had been cleaned up, the broken glass swept away, books returned to shelves, and new slipcovers were in place to hide the slashed cushions on the sofa and chairs. New furniture would have to wait until the legal bills were all paid and Silver Bells had bounced back. This season had been costly in more ways than one, and Natalie knew that it would probably take years to recoup her losses.

But tonight was not the time to dwell on all that. She reached over and ruffled Kyle's hair. "The sooner you get into bed and go to sleep, the sooner he'll come."

"But I wanna see him!"

Natalie shook her head. "It doesn't work that way. Now scoot on off to bed. I'll be there in a minute to tuck you in."

He gave her a quick hug, then tore off toward his bedroom, his excitement an almost-tangible thing. Natalie wanted to savor this moment. Kyle was six years old. By next year, he might not even believe in Santa anymore, and once that happened, once the magic was gone, Christmas would never be the same.

She sighed, thinking about Spence. Where was he tonight? How was he spending Christmas Eve? Alone in the Bishop mansion? Alone in some hotel room?

Or had he already gone back to Washington? Had he already put Natalie out of his mind?

And Kyle? Would Spence forget him, too? Pretend that he had never learned the truth?

Or would he want to be a part of Kyle's life? Would he want to claim his son? Would he want to take Kyle away from her?

Natalie didn't think he would. He wasn't that kind of man. But the fact remained that she had had Kyle for six years and Spence hadn't. If she were in his place, what would she do?

It wasn't an easy question to answer, and when the doorbell rang, Natalie was glad for the interruption. Thinking it must be her parents, she swung the door wide, then froze.

Spence stood on her porch, one hand propped against the door frame. The black leather jacket, the dark hair, the shadow of a beard all combined to make him look a bit on the sinister side.

Natalie's heart thudded as they stood staring at each other for a moment. Then, without a word, she stepped back for him to enter. He brushed past her, bringing a cold draft into the room. Natalie shivered as she closed the door and turned to face him.

"I suppose you're wondering what I'm doing here," he said, looking grim.

"I . . . thought you probably came to see Kyle."

"I would like to see him."

"He's already in bed," she said, wondering if that was the real reason he'd come. The only reason.

As if reading her mind, Spence said, "I've made some decisions, and I thought you should hear them."

He looked so determined. So resolute. Natalie's heart dropped.

Before either of them could say another word, Kyle appeared in the doorway. "Mom! I thought you were going to tuck me in—" Then he saw Spence, and his eyes lit. He dashed across the room and launched himself at Spence, catching both Natalie and Spence by surprise.

For a moment, Spence seemed at a loss, then he caught Kyle in his arms and hugged him tightly. His eyes met Natalie's, and try as she might, she couldn't tear her gaze away. The sight of father and son embracing in front of the Christmas tree, just the way she had pictured it so many times, brought hot tears to her eyes.

Spence's eyes looked suspiciously bright, too. He buried his face in Kyle's hair, as if drinking in the very essence of his son. Then Kyle wiggled out of his arms and got down on all fours, gazing intently under the tree.

Natalie cleared her throat. "What are you looking for, sweetie?"

"I thought maybe Santa might have come while I wasn't looking," Kyle said.

"I told you he won't come until you fall asleep." Natalie tried to sound strict, but couldn't quite manage the stern expression to go with it. "Back to bed, young man."

"Can Uncle Spence tuck me in?"

Spence's gaze met hers again. Hurt flashed in his eyes, and Natalie felt his pain all the way to her soul.

"Can he?" Kyle demanded.

"If he wants to," Natalie said softly.

"I'd be honored," Spence said. The two of them disappeared down the hallway, and it was a long time before Spence returned alone.

Natalie had brought in a bottle of wine and two glasses and placed them on the coffee table. She motioned now for him to sit beside her on the sofa. "Would you like a drink?"

One dark eyebrow rose. ''Are you trying to mellow me?''

Natalie's fingers shook slightly as she poured the wine. ''Do I need to?''

''I guess that depends on how you feel about what I have to say.'' He took the wine from her, but set his glass aside without drinking.

Natalie left her own glass untouched as she turned to face him, her heart hammering in her throat. ''You want to tell Kyle the truth,'' she said.

''He has a right to know.''

She nodded, knowing what the truth might do to her son. To the way he felt about her. ''When?''

''When the time is right,'' Spence said, using her own words. ''I'd like to spend some time with him, get to know him better and let him get to know me. I don't want to hurt him, Natalie. That's the last thing I want. But you and I know better than anyone how badly lies can hurt. And in the end, the truth always comes out.''

''So what are you suggesting?'' she asked carefully. ''That I allow him to visit you in Washington?'' He shook his head and Natalie's heart sank. ''You wouldn't—''

''Fight you for custody?'' he asked.

''Please don't—''

''I wouldn't do that. I would never do anything to hurt Kyle. You're his mother, and he loves you. I can see that. You two have a very special relationship. I don't want to take that away from you, Natalie. Not for his sake and not for yours.''

''Then what *do* you want?'' Natalie asked, afraid to know and afraid not to.

Spence shrugged. ''To be a part of that relationship. Maybe in a small way at first, but later, when Kyle gets to know me and you come to trust me, maybe then . . ." His words trailed away as Natalie gave a little gasp of surprise.

She put her fingertips to her lips. "Are you saying that . . . you want to be a part of my life, too?"

"I've never stopped loving you," he said with devastating simplicity.

Natalie closed her eyes as a wave of emotion swept over her. He loved her! After all the lies and secrets and heartache, he still loved her. It was a miracle, too much to hope for. . . .

She felt his touch against her hair and opened her eyes to find herself gazing deeply into his.

"I've put in for a transfer to San Antonio," he said. "I don't want to rush you, Natalie. I want us both to have plenty of time." He smiled—a bittersweet, poignant smile. "After all, when you think about it, we hardly even know each other. You may not even like me."

"But I'll always love you," she said.

Something changed in his expression—a softening that took her breath away. "Well, that's something, isn't it? After all we've been through."

"It's everything," Natalie said softly.

He picked up the wineglasses and handed one to her.

"Merry Christmas," Natalie whispered.

"Happy Birthday," he said.

The crystal chimed gently as they touched glasses. Their lips met, but only briefly, as if they both were afraid the wonderful spell that had been cast upon them could be too easily broken.

"There's something I've been wondering about," Natalie said hesitantly. "But I don't know if this is the right time to ask you."

"What is it?"

"The night my house was ransacked ... you told me your father had cut you out of his will."

A cloud passed over Spence's features, and Natalie reached out to take his hand, to offer him the love and support she'd had to keep hidden for so long.

"What I've been wondering," she continued softly, "is how you managed to post my bail. A quarter of a million dollars is a lot of money."

"Especially for a lowly FBI agent," he said wryly, but his eyes glinted with amusement. "Years ago I bought some land on the outskirts of San Antonio with the last of the money my grandparents left me. The property wasn't worth much then, and Anthony laughed at my investment. I guess he didn't figure on the city spreading so fast. Or that I might have a little more sense than he gave me credit for. Anyway, that same property is now a pretty valuable piece of real estate. I used it as collateral to secure a bank loan."

Natalie gazed at him in wonder. "You did that for me? What if I'd skipped town? You would have lost everything."

He looked back at her, his gaze deep and intense. "If you'd left town, the money would have been the least of my losses."

"Oh, Spence." She squeezed his hand, her eyes brimming with tears.

"Look," he said and pointed to the window behind her. Outside, in the glow of the porch light, something white drifted downward.

They both got up and went to the window. Snowflakes danced in the moonlight, twirling toward the stillwarm ground, where they melted almost instantly.

Two days ago, it had been eighty degrees. And now it was snowing!

"I can't believe it," Natalie said, laughing with delight. "When do you suppose was the last time it snowed on Christmas Eve in San Antonio?"

"I don't know," Spence replied. "Maybe never. But it's only a few flurries. It'll never stick."

"I don't care," Natalie said softly. "I still think it's a miracle."

"I've never believed in miracles." Spence's arm slipped around her waist and he drew her close. "Until now..."

COMING NEXT MONTH

#401 MAN WITHOUT A BADGE by Dani Sinclair
Lawman
Something about Sam Moore seemed suspicious, but Marly Kramer
was in desperate need of a strong, hardy horseman to help with her
farm. Unfortunately, as soon as she began to fall for Sam, she started
suspecting the truth—that he'd come, not for her, but for a young
child she was sworn to protect....

#402 A NEW YEAR'S CONVICTION by Cassie Miles
Eyewitness
The Witness Protection Program gave Maggie Deere a fresh start—
until Travis Shanahan called her back to New Orleans for a murderer's
retrial. The sexy prosecutor was determined to protect the new
Maggie—even if it meant taking the law into his own hands.

#403 NO WAY OUT by Tina Vasilos
Jenny Gray had secret reasons for entering Theo Zacharias's life, so
she hadn't expected to be so attracted to the man. Nor did she expect
him to want her. With so much romance in the air, Jenny hardly knew
how to tell Theo the dangerous truth...that she'd accidentally delivered the hit money for a murder...his!

#404 THE DEFENDANT by Gay Cameron
Legal Thriller
With her young son, attorney Audrey McKenna excitedly returned to
her hometown of Tabbs Corner, Virginia, to start fresh. But then she
learned her first client would be none other than Conner Hastings.
Years ago she'd silently vowed never to tell him she carried his child.
Now would her secret destroy any chance she had of proving his inno-
cence...and of getting him back?

AVAILABLE THIS MONTH:

#397 A MAN OF SECRETS
Amanda Stevens

#398 PROTECT ME, LOVE
Alice Orr

#399 A CHRISTMAS KISS
Caroline Burnes

#400 BABY IN MY ARMS
Madeline Harper

Look us up on-line at: http://www.romance.net

HARLEQUIN ®

Scandals

A passionate story of romance, where bold, daring characters set out to defy their world of propriety and strict social codes.

"Scandals—a story that will make your heart race and your pulse pound. Spectacular!" —Suzanne Forster

"Devon is daring, dangerous and altogether delicious." —Amanda Quick

Don't miss this wonderful full-length novel from Regency favorite Georgina Devon.

Available in December, wherever Harlequin books are sold.

HARLEQUIN®

I N T R I G U E®

In steamy New Orleans, three women witnessed the same crime, testified against the same man and were then swept into the Witness Protection Program. But now, there's new evidence. These three women are about to come out of hiding—and find both danger and desire....

Start your new year right with all the books in the exciting EYEWITNESS miniseries:

#399 A CHRISTMAS KISS
by Caroline Burnes (December)

#402 A NEW YEAR'S CONVICTION
by Cassie Miles (January)

#406 A VALENTINE HOSTAGE
by Dawn Stewardson (February)

Don't miss these three books—or miss out on all the passion and drama of the crime of the century!

◆HARLEQUIN®

Don't miss these Harlequin favorites by some of our most distinguished authors! And now you can receive a discount by ordering two or more titles!

HT#25657	PASSION AND SCANDAL by Candace Schuler	$3.25 U.S $3.75 CAN.	☐ ☐
HP#11787	TO HAVE AND TO HOLD by Sally Wentworth	$3.25 U.S. $3.75 CAN.	☐ ☐
HR#03385	THE SISTER SECRET by Jessica Steele	$2.99 U.S. $3.50 CAN	☐ ☐
HS#70634	CRY UNCLE by Judith Arnold	$3.75 U.S. $4.25 CAN.	☐ ☐
HI#22346	THE DESPERADO by Patricia Rosemoor	$3.50 U.S. $3.99 CAN	☐ ☐
HAR#16610	MERRY CHRISTMAS, MOMMY by Muriel Jensen	$3.50 U.S. $3.99 CAN.	☐ ☐
HH#28895	THE WELSHMAN'S WAY by Margaret Moore	$4.50 U.S. $4.99 CAN.	☐ ☐

(limited quantities available on certain titles)

AMOUNT	$
DEDUCT: 10% DISCOUNT FOR 2+ BOOKS	$
POSTAGE & HANDLING	$
($1.00 for one book, 50¢ for each additional)	
APPLICABLE TAXES*	$_____
TOTAL PAYABLE	$_____

(check or money order—please do not send cash)

To order, complete this form and send it, along with a check or money order for the total above, payable to Harlequin Books, to: In the U.S.: 3010 Walden Avenue, P.O. Box 9047, Buffalo, NY 14269-9047; In Canada: P.O. Box 613, Fort Erie, Ontario, L2A 5X3.

Name: _____

Address: _____ City: _____

State/Prov.: _____ Zip/Postal Code: _____

*New York residents remit applicable sales taxes.
 Canadian residents remit applicable GST and provincial taxes.   HBACK-OD3

Look us up on-line at: http://www.romance.net

1997

Reader's Engagement Book
A calendar of important dates
and anniversaries for readers to use!

Informative and entertaining—with notable
dates and trivia highlighted throughout the year.

Handy, convenient, pocketbook size to help you
keep track of your own personal important dates.

Added bonus—contains $5.00 worth of coupons
for upcoming Harlequin and Silhouette books.
This calendar more than pays for itself!

Available beginning in November at
your favorite retail outlet.

The collection of the year!
NEW YORK TIMES BESTSELLING AUTHORS

Linda Lael Miller
Wild About Harry

Janet Dailey
Sweet Promise

Elizabeth Lowell
Reckless Love

Penny Jordan
Love's Choices

and featuring
Nora Roberts
The Calhoun Women

This special trade-size edition features four of the wildly
popular titles in the Calhoun miniseries together in
one volume—a true collector's item!

Pick up these great authors and a chance to win
a weekend for two in New York City at the
Marriott Marquis Hotel on Broadway! We'll pay
for your flight, your hotel—even a Broadway show!

Available in December at your favorite retail outlet.

NEW YORK
Marriott.
MARQUIS

HARLEQUIN® Silhouette®

NYT1296-R

FREE VALENTINE'S BROOCH! $9.95 U.S. retail value

This Valentine's Day Harlequin brings you all the essentials—romance, chocolate and jewelry—in:

VALENTINE Delights

Matchmaking chocolate-shop owner Papa Valentine dispenses sinful desserts, mouth-watering chocolates...and advice to the lovelorn, in this collection of three delightfully romantic stories by Meryl Sawyer, Kate Hoffmann and Gina Wilkins.

As our special Valentine's Day gift to you, each copy of *Valentine Delights* will have a beautiful, filigreed, heart-shaped brooch attached to the cover.

Make this your most delicious Valentine's Day ever with *Valentine Delights!*

Available in February wherever Harlequin books are sold.

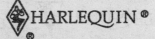

HARLEQUIN ®

VAL97